E

A Novella
Part 1

By, T. A. Walker

Copyright© 2017
T. A. Walker

For Danny

I

"Wake me up, before you go, go. Don't leave me hanging on like a yo-yo. Wake me up."

I silence my iPhone and launch out of bed. I hate everything on the planet right now.

Senior year is none of the fun everybody promised it would be. Instead of fun, I have to go to work and maintain my GPA so I don't screw up my chance at Oxford.

A text message flashes on my lock screen from Easton High.

Report to the main office in place of your zero hour class this morning. You will receive further instructions when you arrive.

My mind blanks. I am no stranger to the principal's office, but I've been an angel, so far.

What I could've done wrong nags me the entire drive to school.

My fears finally go away when the administrative secretary smiles at me. Horn and I aren't exactly on smiling terms. I've been to the office too many times for her to pretend that she likes me.

I'm a straight-A student, but in the past, I was always in trouble. It turns out that teachers don't like disrespect no matter what kind of grades you make.

Every week, Mr. Webb sat across from me, shaking his head.

"I know that I don't have to tell you that I am disappointed that such a bright young lady like you can't control herself." He would begin.

I always looked down at my hands. He had heard every excuse from me a trillion times. I was there to listen only. Arguing with him was pointless, so I took his prattle as part of my punishment.

It wasn't long before Mr. Webb grew on me. I could tell he liked me too. He was the only administrator who wanted to understand me. He never condoned my behavior, but he always told me how bright I was. He always said that by thirty; I'd be unstoppable.

Mr. Webb would never see me at thirty, or even eighteen. He died of a massive heart attack over the summer.

The news that Mr. Webb died changed me. I stopped challenging my teachers to the point of disrespect. Now, I only answer questions asked of me. Not only am I better behaved, but Co-op rescues me from any trouble that I could get in.

"You look lovely with your hair like that." Horn remarks. Her dull gray eyes stare at me approvingly over the top her turquoise framed glasses. She never makes small talk with me. Not pleasant small talk anyway.

I slide a hand over my new short hairstyle.

She continues, "I wish I could get away with that." She pushes her box blonde curly do up at the temples.

"Thank you," I try.

A shrill ring screams in the empty office.

Hendrat could've just opened his door and called me in, but that would be too easy. His name isn't Hendrat, but the students refuse to tarnish Hendrix's name by associating him with this guy.

"I'll send her in. Go on in, Zoe." Horn says as if I there's any other possible person who he's calling for.

I force my body into his overpowering pine-scented office. When Mr. Webb was here, it always smelled like Hazelnut coffee.

"Good morning, Zoe. How do you do?"

"Fine." I look down at the chair in front of his desk, hoping he'll catch on.

He's so clueless. Mr. Webb always greeted his visitors in the waiting area. He also waited until his visitor sat down before he sat his rotund belly behind his desk.

"Please do have a seat, Ms. Mason." Hendrat remembers.

I don't know how he even knows it's me, the way he's furiously scribbling on his legal pad.

"The message I got this morning said I should report here in place of zero hour?" I nag him.

He looks up quickly, nods his head, and then hunches over his legal pad again.

"It didn't say much else about why I should come to the office," I continue. This guy is about to make me blemish the best month of school I've had in three years.

"That is correct, I'm finishing up a couple of things." The tip of his tongue peeks out the corner of his mouth like a five-year-old practicing his letters.

At last, he snaps the tab on his black pen and then sits up like a rod's stuck up his ass.

"You are aware of our foreign exchange student policy?" His ice blue eyes make him look like a fresh vampire, and not the sexy Brad Pitt kind.

"Not really," I throw out.

"Very well." He pulls out a drawer and rambles through it until he finds a laminated booklet. He pushes it across his desk.

I stare at it, and then look back up at him.

"Please turn to page 15." He nods down at the document.

I resist the urge to snatch it off the desk.

"As a smart student like you has already deduced, you will be chaperoning this year." He announces.

"I can't be a chaperone. I'm only here for half a day." I argue.

He silences me with his long fingers up.

"I am well aware of that." He remarks.

I hate how his blue dress shirt matches his blood-thirsty eyes so well.

"It is beneficial for you to chaperone him, even if it is for a partial day. You are the top student in your graduating class and he is the top student from his former school."

I don't care. "Don't I get a say in this?"

He smiles, but his evil eyes don't. "Don't doubt yourself, Ms. Mason." He fishes around on his desk until he locates a blue folder. "I see you have three extra credits. You've had the top GPA since you started here in 2013. You also have quite the active disciplinary record." He slides the folder down far enough for me to notice his threat.

I don't bat an eyelash. Hopefully, he read the part where I ate idiots like him from breakfast in past years.

"Some may see your discipline record as a social academic disqualification." He allows his son subtle threat to hang in the air. "I don't. I regard it as a sign that you are an excellent multi-tasker. Besides, I have no reason to believe that you will be a repeat offender this year. The summer has been quite good for you." He closes his case.

I swallow down what he can do with his blue folder and exhale slowly. "Who's the new student?" I bite out.

His sinister smile knows he's won.

"Very good. His name is Azem Farak, and he's from East Jerusalem.

My stomach acid churns counterclockwise with every line he recites.

"For reference sake, it is best to inform you that he has a Muslim background. But he is very open about his conversion to Christianity." Hendrix assures.

"Why are you telling me all this?" I demand.

Mr. Hendrix pulls at the collar on the blood red noose around his neck. "This is important to know, he punctuates," in case, you students confront bullying. You know that we have a zero-tolerance policy for such behavior.

Should you have such an experience, I urge you to report it to the office at once." Instructs Mr. Hendrix.

"Oh my God," I palm my face.

"I'm sorry what was that?"

I shake my head. "Nothing," I answer.

"Ms. Mason, there is no need for concern. I assure you that this is all standard procedure. Every chaperone undergoes the same briefing process."

"What time is he coming?"

"He starts tomorrow. Report to the office tomorrow instead of zero hour. Until then, read over our Foreign Exchange Manual and I'll see you in the morning." He resumes scribbling on his legal pad, effectively dismissing me from his office.

II

"Mom, that's all he said." I shrug.

"So you sat in his office and all he said was that he was from East Jerusalem?" Mom yells out on her way to her room. She breaks back into my room and plops down on my bed.

"Mom," I warn.

"What? You need to know what to expect." She flips the top up and pecks around the keyboard. "Come here." She flicks her head over.

I drag my over to the bed and sit next to her. I pretend to watch the virtual guide she found.

"Did you see that?" She draws up to the screen until the all I can see is her spiral curls.

"Mom, I'm showing him where his classes are, not marrying him."

She stops clicking around the screen and looks at me. "You don't sound very excited." She notices.

"Would you be?" I say.

"Hey, I'm trying to help you, don't be disrespectful." She closes her laptop.

"I know mom, I'm sorry. I had a shi... bad day." I correct.

Her lips curl up at the edges. "You're not too big for a spanking," she threatens.

"Please." I counter.

"Oh, you're tough now?" She challenges.

"I didn't say it, you did." I inch toward my door, and take off before she can slide her laptop off her lap. Despite my head start, she's still on my tail.

I scream and hurtle through her bedroom door and into the bed. She jumps in after me. She strangles my foot and does the one thing I hate.

"What did you say you were going to do?"

"Ok, mom, stop!"

"What's the magic word?" She scales my feet with her claw length nails.

"You're the most beautiful mother in the world." I shriek.

She releases me, and I leap up.

"And don't forget it." She laughs.

"I bought some blueberry muffins. There are some of those microwavable sausage links in the freezer for breakfast." She combs her fingertips through her hair.

"Thanks."

"I'll call you when I get to work." She says five minutes later.

"Didn't you just get off a few hours ago?" I snap my Calculus III book closed.

"I told you I was standing in for Mary." She taps her knee.

"Uh, no you didn't." I declare.

"Zo, I don't have time to argue with you about it right now. I've got to go. Call if you need me." She darts out my room and hustles out the house.

Mom is the only nurse I know that works harder than the entire staff at Chicago Regional Hospital. Her co-workers must love her since she loves picking up the hours they ditch.

Nursing is the only job I've known her to have. Before dad died, she made nursing look fun. Now, I hate hospitals. The way she idolizes that place makes me sick to my stomach.

Why she thinks she's solving anything by avoiding being here with me I don't know. Dad's been gone for six years. I know he was her husband, but he was my dad, and I can barely remember how he looks. It's not a fact that I'm proud of, but every year he's gone, the picture of his face in my mind blurs a little bit more. One of my biggest fears is that one day his face will be gone altogether.

Maybe I didn't have room enough to cry, with the devastated state my mom was in. For the first two years, I was my mom's mom. The stuff I had to do to help her, are things that permanently turned me off from health care. No child should ever have to bathe and feed a parent. Taking care of her felt like a sentence for some crime that I don't remember committing.

Then one morning, like the sun coming up over the horizon, her mourning was over. She literally got out of the bed, and resumed life, like she was Rip Van Winkle.

I was so happy to have her back. I didn't care about being mad any more. Anything was better than tiptoeing into her room and talking to myself. My skin crawled every time I had to beg her to open up a little bit more so I wouldn't keep spilling soup down her chin.

To the world at large, Claire Mason was back. Her light brown skin was fresh. Her hair was always styled within an inch of its life, and her makeup was flawless. They saw a beautiful black woman, who knew her shit about nursing, but all I saw was a living corpse.

The only thing mom snapped out of was living in a catatonic, prone position. Going back to Regional was an ingenious way for her to never have to engage in my life in any significant way again. The graveyard shift kept her work and home life blurred, and her bed barely slept in.

At one point I almost suggested that she try dating again, but I couldn't risk her shutting down on me again. A living corpse was better than a dead one.

When I got to high school, my absentee mother, earned me major cred. I could do whatever I wanted, while everyone else scrambled to meet curfew on school nights. By the time mom made it home the next morning, she had no idea what I had done the night before. I could've spent the night gambling in Vegas for all she knew. Embarrassingly enough, I was home studying most nights. There were plenty of times where I had to jump in the bed fully clothed with the covers up to my chin so I wouldn't get caught.

The academic in me knows that I should take mom's rare sage advice, and research this kid's previous home. But that creates more homework for me, and no thank you. He's the one who should be studying what life is like here. Hendrat forcing me to babysit him feels like some kind of punishment. This is probably the best way he can pay me back for all the crap on my disciplinary file. Knowing him, he would probably love to see me slide back into my old ways again.

The longer I think about it, the more I'm convinced it must be true. Another top student could've easily been selected, but no he picks me. That asshat knows that I need a scholarship to Oxford like I need to breathe every day.

For all the work she does, mom never has any money. Every time I ask her for money she says is that she can't even afford to pay attention.

For all her nagging about how I need a scholarship before I can see the hallway in a college, she does nothing to help. The only thing she gives me, free of charge, of course, is a nice shooting down of every out of state college I want to go to.

I gave up sharing my dreams of going to Oxford last year. She had a fit when I casually slipped in that I wanted to go out of state to college.

"Out of the question." She slammed the corner of orange juice in her glass and walked it to the sink.

"Mom, you won't have to pay for anything," I explained.

"Zoe, I am not playing with you. You do not have my permission to leave this state, and even in-state you can only go so far away. You are my baby, and I won't have you leaving me." She swished water in her glass.

"Mom, I'm coming back to visit."

She slammed the glass down.

"Shit, Zo, look what you made me do." She cradled her dripping hand.

"Oh, my God, mom, let me see it."

"Go to school, and don't bring up some damned Oxford to me again. We will talk about all of that when the time comes. You might not even want to do all that this time next year." She wrapped the dishrag around her hand like a tourniquet.

It was hard to argue with her with a soaked hand, but she couldn't have been more wrong.

A year later, and I'm no closer to convincing her that Oxford is where I want to go to college. At this point, I'm not sure if I even care about where I go to college anymore. As long as it's away from here, I could be happy, even though I'm not sure I remember how it feels. There are days when switching to full time at my job and moving out feels like a dream come true.

I select Ferris Bueller's Day Off on the Guide and wish that I could skip the whole thing tomorrow. Having the honor of adding ink to my lengthy discipline record would make Hendrat's life.

I drive the volume on the TV up loud enough to drown everything else out. Somehow all those creepy sounds that visit when I'm alone disappear when mom's here.

Before I doze off, I pray that this kid knows Basic English. If he does, I plan on having him out of my hair by the end of the week.

III

I'm so glad that this kid doesn't have to follow me around while everybody's watching, yet. The school doesn't fill up until a few minutes before the eight thirty bell.

I drag through the entrance to the office.

Hendrat's door is open, so I skip the fake smiles with Horn and head inside.

"Bright and early." Hendrat coos.

I fail at smiling and look around his drab office.

"I like to see you so eager Ms. Mason, but you've beaten him here." He shoots up from his seat, buttons the middle button on his tweed blazer, and steps around his desk.

Under threat of gunfire, I could admit that his clothes aren't bad; it's his ora that ruins everything. There isn't a genuine thing about him unless you count the raw spite behind every word he says.

I steal a seat after he exits the office. My purse vibrates.

How's it going? A text from mom says.

I don't know yet.

Send me a pic, when you do. She responds.

I turn my phone off.

Heaviness gathers behind me.

I slam my eyes shut before I stand to my feet and face my sentence.

A tall, fair-skinned man stands next to Hendrat.

The three of us trade curious stares like we're playing visual ping pong.

I've almost had it with waiting for this kid to get here. Can't they call me down to the office when he figures out how to get to the school?

The tall guy's thick, black hair, falls over his brow when he looks down at his black Jordan's.

Whatever the hell he's here for, he's cute as hell. It's a shame he has to do business with Hendrat.

"Zoe Mason, Azem, Farak. Azem Farak, Zoe Mason." Hendrat zips between us for his desk.

I follow him over; the confusion is plain on my face. This can't be right.

"Hello." Azem's voice says inching toward me.

I face him and shake his outstretched hand.

I can't stop marveling at how good his razor-sharp haircut and crisp clothes look.

Hendrat shuffles back over and hands us two pieces of paper.

"I've printed a schedule for you so that you'll have no problems finding Mr. Farak." Hendrat smiles tightly. His wooden smile always reminds me of a ventriloquist's dummy.

"I have every confidence that your senior year will be a wonderful one." Hendrat herds us over to the door.

I have no idea what to do with all this fine standing next to me. I expected him to be a blithering idiot following me around, not the other way around.

"Good day students." Hendrat opens the door wider so we can both step through. Once out, he snaps the door shut and clicks the lock.

"Damn," Azem says to Hendrat's door.

I try my best to keep a straight face, but it's something I would say if I could find my brains. Azem's wit doesn't seem like it was born two worlds away.

Azem turns around and looks down at me.

He smiles.

I join him, despite wanting to be nonchalant. It is impossible to look at his brilliant face and have a negative reaction.

I rip my eyes away from his and scan his schedule. I can't concentrate on it, but that doesn't matter. I have to do something to stop staring at him.

The longer he stares down at me, waiting for me to do something, the more self-conscious I get.

It didn't dawn on me to care about what I wore today. As his chaperone, I should've at least worn a blouse and sandals, instead of a tunic tank, skinnies, and Chuck's. He's only wearing a gray t-shirt and black jeans, but his body makes the fabric look so good.

I clear my throat and search for some confidence.

"Let's go." I step in front of him and exit the main office.

He follows close behind.

I can feel his gaze on me, even though I can't be sure.

Facing away from him is much easier than confronting his bright eyes.

Before I look like an ass for leading him on a wild goose chase, I actually read his schedule.

"This way." I double back to the East hall for the basement steps.

A soft laugh from him behind me makes me break out in a sweat.

I shake it off and keep walking. If he is laughing at me, I deserve it. I'm acting like I've never seen a guy before, and it's embarrassing.

Something about him makes me keep our shared first hour a secret. I can't take him snickering at me again.

"That's it. The higher up you go, the higher the classroom number. You should be able to find your classes by yourself after today." I glance at him.

His eyes bear down on me.

"I don't know if I can understand that as easily as you put it." He crinkles his brow at his schedule.

This guy is trolling me, and it's not funny.

I roll my eyes.

His cherry blushed lips make me bite my bottom lip.

"I'm supposed to have a chaperone, and I expect to have one." He beams at me.

"You can handle it." I insist.

His square jaw flexes as his smile goes more vivid than it already is. He saddles up close to me. "I thought this was going be terrible, but if I knew it was going to be like this, I could have saved myself a lot of worrying." He admits.

If I had his courage I would admit the same to him. Instead, I look over his schedule for the millionth time. It freaks me out that I already have his schedule memorized.

He twists his body from side to side before he asks me, "Do you mind leading the way to first hour as you call it, again? I don't quite understand your numbering system yet." He says.

We arrive at Calculus III before any of the class arrives. MacGregor thumbs the lens of his glasses with corner of his shirt. I try to dump Azem at his desk.

"Don't leave Ms. Mason."

I blanch, and then back up to his desk.

"We should sit, Mr. Farak, is it? MacGregor enunciates.

Azem nods.

"Right behind you. We'll move John to the third row."

I throw my head back.

Azem snickers all the way to his seat.

I don't hear a syllable Mac Gregor says for wondering what Azem thinks about my non-revelation. Besides that, I wish cared about more than how my ass looks in my jeans every day. I never take the time to check anything else. My hair's so short, that it's easy for me to overlook it all together most days.

The whole time MacGregor lectures the class back to sleep, I calculate how popular Azem's going to be. By the end of first hour, everybody who matters will know who he is. I steal peeks around the class and notice students sneaking texts. The texting train has already left the station, and won't stop until they know everything. Somehow this phenomenon rarely gets anything wrong, at first. By this time next month, ninety-nine percent of the texts about him will be fan fiction. The creative stories can last for weeks at a time. The only time the story stops is when the harassed student's parents complain.

Azem's arrival will trigger the whole school. Nobody's ever cared about previous exchange students. An exchange student like Azem will have students begging to be chaperones.

When the bell rings, I'm ashamed at myself for checking out the whole time. It's a good thing that MacGregor's as predictable as the minute hand on a clock. I'm so glad that our assignments are always consecutive, or I'd have to ask Azem for the homework. Not a good look.

Azem's feet tap leg of my chair.

I turn around and try to ignore the way everyone staring at us.

Azem doesn't seem to notice that all eyes are on him. He packs his book bag, and stands next to my desk, and waits for me to pack up.

By lunchtime, I'm mentally exhausted.

I can't walk two paces without popular girls asking me for Azem's number. I would understand if they'd ever said two words to me in the past, but I expected as much.

I'm so desperate to hide from my newfound fame, that I take him to the darker, more secluded part of the cafeteria. It isn't until I take in the couples around me that I realize I've made another mistake.

If Hendrat wouldn't have forced me to take off work, I could be gone right now. Instead, I'm sitting in the couple's corner, with my stomach twisting into a double knot.

"Where's your food?" Azem asks after he parks his tray on the table.

"I'm not hungry." I read the same of Rebecca for the fourth time.

"Come here." He pushes one of the two remaining chairs toward me.

I bookmark my page, and then lock my phone.

"What?" This guy's not going to let me off the hook until I've served my time.

"Come here." He urges.

I slide over to the chair, and he pulls it even closer.

Azem halves his turkey sandwich and divides the sweet potato fries. The pile of fries closest to me sits taller than his.

"Don't move." Azem darts from the table for the cash register.

He asks the cashier for a cup and she gives him three. She refuses to take back the extras. He returns to our table and pours half of his Dasani water into the triple stack. He caps the bottle and pushes it toward me.

I can't breathe.

"Eat up. This stuff is already gross, don't eat it cold." He stuffs a bounty of fries into his mouth.

"Thank you for today," Azem says after he swallows.

He's so sincere, that I have to stop chewing.

"You're welcome."

"I know it's annoying to have to do this." He hands me a napkin, then wipes his cherry kissed lips. "I'm kind of rubbing it in, so I'm sorry for that." He confesses.

"It's ok," I can't believe the words coming out of my mouth right now.

"If you don't want to, you don't have to chaperone me tomorrow. I won't say a word." He pushes his pointer finger into his lips. I envy his finger.

I want to be his chaperone so bad now I can taste it like the sweet potato fry I jam into my mouth. He can't be firing me right now.

"With my luck, Mr. Hendrix will find out, and I'll have to hear about it. I'll ask him how long I have to do this, so we don't have any problems." It hurts my soul to name Hendrat properly, but I can't afford for it come back to bite me.

He's resting his cheek on his fist staring at me intensely.

"What caused you to cut your hair?"

My fingers drift to the nape of my neck. My hair's shorter than it's ever been, but I love it. I shrug although I know exactly what gave me the courage to do it. Whatever snapped in me after Mr. Webb died made me throw caution away this summer. Thankfully, my wild disregard only went as far as a haircut. I doubt I would've loved any other wild decisions half as much as I love this one.

"You should keep it like that." Says Azem.

"Why?"

"Because it's really sexy on you, that's why. See you tomorrow Zoe." Azem swipes his mouth, and then drops his napkin on the tray.

We have to walk together for the trashcan. He turns back afterward. Something inside of me wants to walk back to the table with him, but I can't make myself do it.

I blindly cross the school parking lot and a busy intersection to get to my car on the commuter lot.

As happy as I was that Hendrat allowed me to keep my half-day status, I'm disappointed now.

Hendrat claimed that it's better for Azem to get used to me leaving every day. According to him, today's lunch was imperative for his social introduction. For all Hendrat's social preaching, he wasn't very social when he kicked us out of his office this morning.

Every time Azem's compliment echoes in my memory I have to grip the steering wheel tighter.

All the other guys at school lust over the Rapunzel hair every other girl wears. I could understand it if the hair the guys loved was real, but most of it isn't.

The first time Raina's spoken more than two words to me is when she noticed my new hairstyle. In her cosmetology obsessed mind, my hair length is best for wig wear.

When we were friends, she couldn't fathom that I was serious about hating hair extensions. She always blew me off when I told her that I liked the hair I was born with.

Hair was the least of our differences.

The tech-school crowd she worshipped turned her into someone I didn't know. For three years we were tight, now, we ignore each other when we cross paths in the hallways.

Thinking back, it's amazing that we ever became friends. She slathered her face with makeup every day, despite a perfect complexion.

She had nothing but contempt for the minimal mascara, eyeliner, and lip gloss that I wore.

Mom told me that makeup should play up my best features, not transform me into Bozo the clown. When I asked her who Bozo the clown was, she hunted for a clip on the Internet.

Images of the scary clown were enough to drive her point home.

When Raina continued to rail on about my preschool makeup choices, I let it go right out the other ear.

I almost showed her the YouTube clip of Bozo, but I didn't want to change her.

I hope Azem doesn't have the same feelings about my makeup choices. I am almost eighteen. Maybe I should know how to plaster on foundation and highlighter by now.

Mom grills me about Azem but I fake having too much homework.

A much as I hate it, I have to give it to Hendrat. Today was the ultimate checkmate. There's no possible way I could've prepared for Azem. Hendrat had to have a picture of Azem in his file, but he chose to keep it a secret.

I cleanse my face and brush my teeth. As I study my face in the bathroom mirror, I will myself to forget about how embarrassing today was. I flick the switch off in the bathroom and dive into bed.

It doesn't matter that Azem's strong upper body, makes a t-shirt look so good. I curl up in my comforter. I have to free one of my legs when I think about how right his jeans lay at his pelvis. I turn the volume up on the TV and lay down. So what if his face looks like it was torn out of a magazine. People come in all varieties. Azem happens to fall in the sexiest man alive category, big deal. Just l like I told him, I can handle it.

I am expected to be a leader, and that's what I'm going to do. Easton is my school. I have to regain control of this situation. I shouldn't be freaking out like some little freshman that doesn't know anything. I'm the top student in the school. I was chosen out of thousands of students. It's about time I started acting like I'm in charge.

I refold my pillow and prop it under my ear.

My eyes slam shut, but before I can remember that I'm the boss, Azem's face bids me a good night.

IV

If only Azem's first day at Easton could've been on Monday, my plans might have a fighting chance.

Instead, I have two whole days to keep this strong front up.

I've never been happy to go to work until now.

I crash after my shift Friday night. The only thing I can think about after work is scrubbing the scent of onions off my skin.

After an extra long shower, I toss my uniform in the washing machine.

I'm in the perfect mood to let Netflix chill and watch me. I hit play, and an unlabeled number texts me.

I forget all about how dog tired I am when I see who it's from.

FaceTime? Azem.

My eyes get as big as the funny cat's on Shrek.

Never mind how he got my number.

I scramble to get camera ready.

I layer on Strawberry Sorbet EOS until my lips gleam. I swipe away the greasy residue that falls outside my lip line. I dig at the corners of my eyes for crust then scramble to make my bed up.

I sit tall against my buttoned pillow headboard. I text him back.

"*Sure.*" I text back.

Azem calls.

When his face fills the screen of my phone, I freeze.

He's laying with an arm behind his head on his bed. His relaxed body makes me loosen up.

"Hi," Azem says.

I cut my smile short. "How did you get my number?"

"I told Hendrat that I would feel more comfortable if I could call you if I needed your help," Azem says.

I can't make my mind up whether I should be mad or thankful for Hendrat parsing out my personal information. I yelp before I can catch myself.

"What?" Azem says.

"You work fast if you already know Hendrat's nickname."

Azem lights up. "How sad for Jimi Hendrix." He says.

"I know. It's so unfair." I say.

"I can hang up if you're not comfortable with me calling you," Says Azem.

"I'm still on the phone," I say.

"But do you want to be?" Azem says.

I roll my eyes.

"Your beautiful eyes are going to get stuck like that."

I catch myself before I roll my eyes again.

Azem notices and cracks up.

I catch a massive yawn.

"Do I bore you that much?" He smiles.

I shake my head. "No, I just got off work."

"Oh. I'll let you rest." Says Azem.

"No, I'm fine. I wouldn't have agreed to FaceTime if I was too tired."

"Whatever you say." He shifts the phone so he can lay on his side. "Do you have a boyfriend Zoe?"

"No," I answer against my will.

"Why not?" Says Azem.

"Do you have a girlfriend?" I counter.

"Have you ever heard, never answer a question with a question?"

"I don't need one," I say.

"That doesn't answer why you don't have one." He reminds me.

"I'm not focused on that right now. Is that ok with you?" I say.

"It'll do for now." He smiles.

"What about you?"

He runs his hand over his hair, and his bicep flexes.

I kick the covers off of my burning feet.

"No, I don't have a girlfriend. Until recently, I haven't found anyone interesting enough to want one." He looks at me without wavering.

A group of shivers run up and down my stomach.

For the next 15 minutes, we talk about a whole lot of nothing, and I enjoy every second of it.

He misses home.

I can sense his turmoil, but I'm too nervous to ask him about it.

There isn't a lull in our conversation until he hits me with something that I'm not prepared for.

"I like you, Zoe," Azem says out of nowhere.

"I like you too." I chew my thumb nail.

He laughs. "Do you work tomorrow?"

I shake my head.

"Can I take you somewhere?" Azem says.

"Why?"

"I told you why already, plus I like being around you."

"I get it now," I say.

"Get what?" Azem questions.

"It's sort of like the Florence Nightingale syndrome. My mom's a nurse, and she's always telling me how her male patients swear that they're in love with her. You only think you like me because I'm the first person you met at school."

He's looking at me like I'm the foreign exchange student. "What time can I pick you up?"

"You tell me," I say.

"I'll be there at 8." He says.

"Ok."

Before we hang up he says, "I hope I can change, your mind about wanting a boyfriend."

Saturday morning, I wear my iPhone like a glove.

Waiting for Azem to call feels like waiting for Christmas.

When he finally texts me, I want to text him right back, but I can't. Instead, I torture myself for two minutes before I text him my address.

I text mom before I get in the shower.

After my shower, I stand in front of my closet until an outfit materializes.

My phone dances across my vanity table.

"Have fun at Raina's."

Mom has no idea that I haven't hung out with Raina since last year.

At seven fifty, the lights from Azem's Audi illuminate the driveway.

I release the blinds in slow motion and pray that he didn't notice me stalking him from my bedroom window.

I want to meet Azem on the porch, but I wait for him to ring the bell.

I love seeing him on the other side of the screen door when I open up. How can he make dark denim jeans and a short-sleeved hoodie look this good?

I step out, and he follows me to his car. He snaps the door tight behind me after I'm inside.

He slides behind the wheel. "Ready to go to the movies?"

The veins in his forearms pop while he backs out the driveway.

"The movies?" I try not to sound disappointed, but it's hard to hold it in. "Nobody goes to the movies anymore," I say.

Azem smiles wide. His sparkling eyes shut my mouth. "You don't go to the movies, for the movie, silly. You go for the atmosphere, and the popcorn."

The thought of being so close to him in a dark theatre makes my stomach flip.

"Your house is nice. I like your neighborhood." Azem's voice reaches inside my mind and yanks me back to the car.

"Thank you. Where do you live?"

"In The Barrows. Have you ever heard of it?" Says Azem.

I have to close my gaping mouth. "Everybody's heard of the Barrows. It's the nicest subdivision in town."

"It's not that nice." Azem rests his arm on the armrest. "Is the air too cold?" He says.

"A little bit," I say, rubbing my arms. If he knew the real reason for my shudder, he would turn the thermostat down more.

Indian summer is my favorite time of the year, especially at night. The warm air tonight is perfect. If I wasn't in the car with Azem, I would let my hand sail in the wind.

I'm glad I chose skinnies and a short-sleeved blouse instead of a dress. I imagine what Azem will do when he notices me shivering in the theater. I shake the thought away and check my lip gloss in the mirrored screen protector on my iPhone.

"I smell cinnamon." Azem leans close to me and sniffs around.

"It's my lip gloss,"

"Does it taste like it too?" Says Azem.

I shift in my seat. "Yes."

He bites his lower lip and I melt a little bit.

When we're a few paces away from the concession counter, Azem nudges me with his shoulder.

"What would you like?"

I shrug.

"Do I have to force feed you every day?" Chides Azem.

"I like slushes,"

"Ok, but you must eat popcorn at the movies. It's the law." He says.

I raise an eyebrow at him.

"Can I help you, sir?" A tall girl with turquoise banded braces says. Her smile is so wide I can see the last brace in her mouth. She tosses her long braids behind one shoulder.

Every muscle in my face is dying to smile like the girl.

He gives her our order, and she zips around behind the counter.

She's so generous with the butter that if her manager was around, she'd be in trouble.

"Enjoy the show, sir." She says.

Azem's eyes flick to her worn nametag. "We will Cassandra."

Cassandra obeys Azem and finally acknowledges me.

There's only one other couple in the theater. They look super uncomfortable with their heads cocked back so far.

Azem guides me to the highest row.

We own the corner.

Azem pulls the armrest divider up so that our seats become one.

He balances the bucket of popcorn on his left thigh and the slush in his right hand.

I attempt to put the slush on the other side of me, but his iron grip doesn't budge.

"I've got it." He insists.

I bend down for a sip, but he stops me.

"Here." He lifts the cup up to my lips.

I pull on the electric blue slush.

Azem takes a swig.

The way he shares the slush with me is so intimate.

Azem licks his lips. "I think you're right, your lip gloss might be cinnamon after all.

"It is cinnamon," I insist.

"I can't be sure." He smiles, and then feeds me more slush.

I'm grateful for the refreshment, but it's doing nothing to douse the flames leaping inside me.

I can't pay attention to the Wayan's brother's latest spoof.

Nothing can top the excitement of eating and drinking with Azem.

"I have 11 brothers," Azem says after he passes the popcorn to me.

I doubt I could take him feeding me the popcorn too.

When he leans over for me to put some in his mouth I almost jump out of my seat. His lips catch the tips of my fingers when he plucks the kernels away.

"Eleven brothers?" I stammer.

"Yep," Azem says.

He stares at my lips while he licks his. "None of them speak to me anymore."

I put the dregs of popcorn on the floor.

Azem drops the slush down in the cup holder next to him.

Another shiver, makes Azem pull me closer to his side.

"Better?" His words tickle my ear and neck.

Say something, Zoe. I nod instead and then try to remember his last line of conversation. "Why won't your brothers speak to you?"

Azem exhales. "Because I left the faith, and they don't want to associate with an apostate. Their lives are in danger if they do."

A chill runs down my spine. "I'm sorry," I say.

"I'm ruining a good time. I will stop." He says.

I shake my head "No you're not. I love talking to you." I confess.

"Not as much as I do." His words heat up my neck.

When I turn around to face him he seizes my lips. His hands capture my face until there's nothing but us. The stronger his stroke of his tongue get, the tighter I wrap my fingers around his hands.

Azem's tongue laps my cheek, then flicks down the slope of my neck. White sparks explode behind my lids while I muffle my mouth.

He kisses my neck one more glorious time before he pulls away from me.

He takes a long sip from the slush, holds it out for me, and then pulls me in again.

After the movie, we go to my job.

I offer to pay, but Azem looks offended that I would make such a suggestion.

Sheila in the drive-thru waves us off when she notices me in the car.

"Please tell me if you have to let one rip, so I can escape." Azem fingers the handle on his door.

I roll my eyes. "Don't worry, I'm immune."

Azem tosses his empty box in the bag.

It's the best dinner I've ever had in my driveway.

I can hear Raina going off about being such a cheap date.

I don't care about that.

Tonight could not have been more romantic.

"Why aren't your siblings here with you and your mom?" I can't believe that all eleven of them feel the same way.

"Because they choose Islam." Says Azem. "According to my dad, I deserve death. He says I should be grateful he couldn't do it himself. Since he's more than up to the task of killing my mom, we had to go."

"I am so sorry, Azem."

The burgers feel like cement in my stomach.

"Don't feel bad for me Zoe. I'm alright." Azem assures me.

I doubt I could be so brave.

"Hopefully one day I'll get through to them." Azem thumbs the corner of my mouth then reaches over the armrest to kiss me.

"What are you doing in twenty minutes?" Azem says on the porch.

"Face Timing you," I say.

He grins, and then kisses me one more time before he leaps down the steps for his car.

"I have a question," I say as soon as Azem's face appears on the screen of my iPhone. "What happens if you have a wife and children one day? Is there an automatic hit out on them too?"

He closes his eyes. "I hope my dad loves me enough not to do anything like that."

"So, is that a yes?" I wish I could stop myself.

"Nothing will ever get to my wife and children. Ever." Azem looks deadly serious. "Thank you for your concern, Zoe. I'm sure my future wife and children will love you for it."

I should be telling him that it was only a hypothetical question.

"When can we go to the movies again?" He says breaking my trance.

All I hear is when can we kiss again. I hunch my shoulders.

"Will I have to wait until school to kiss you again?" Quips Azem.

In all the excitement, I've forgotten that I'm supposed to be his chaperone. I'm almost positive that the handbook doesn't suggest movies and kissing. "I don't know."

The mood of the conversation dips.

"What's wrong?" Azem's even cuter when he's confused.

"I don't want Hendrat to think I'm abusing my position or anything," I say.

The tips of Azem's ears blush red. "I don't give a damn what Hendrat thinks," Azem says.

"I know, but he has access to my transcripts," I reply.

"Ok, we won't kiss anymore then." Says Azem.

My heart deflates. I want to take everything back, but I know it's too late.

Despite the Hendrat hiccup, we stay on the phone until we're dozing off. At some point, I wake up to Azem sleeping on his back. The phone is still pointed at his face. I gawk at him. His sharp jaw line and dark features are unbelievably handsome. He looks so peaceful that instead of waking him up first, I kiss the screen and hang up the phone.

My iPhone pokes into my ribs in the morning. I slide the hot phone from underneath me.

I want to talk to Azem so bad. I don't have the nerve to call him first, so I take a long shower instead. After I'm dressed, I crawl back in bed.

The house is too quiet for my mom to be home. I gave up keeping track of my mom's schedule a long time ago. It seems like she invents reasons to stay at work all day and night.

Only last week, Oxford was my dominating thought.

Now, Azem sits on the throne of my mind. I sit up in bed and command my thoughts to come back to its regularly scheduled programming.

No matter how sexy Azem is, there is no way we can be anything more than kissing buddies. College means too much to me to jeopardize it now. As much as my heart hates it, I have to distance myself from Azem. It has to be better to have a little discomfort now than to fill up an ocean of heartbreak to drown in next summer.

By the time I'm finished brewing a cup of coffee, I feel more like myself.

I grit my teeth through the constant quivering my stomach does every time I flash back to last night.

There's a note on the refrigerator.

"Z, Got called in, won't be off until 6 pm, then going back in for my reg shift @ 9 pm, sorry, see you soon! Love you! P.S. I want to hear all about your mystery student when I get home!"

I roll my eyes and wipe the writing off the mini whiteboard. How can we talk about anything when she'll be power napping?

A shrill ring down the hall makes me sprint to my room. I hear my coffee cup shatter to the floor before I round the corner to rush down the hall.

I pick the phone up off the bed and swipe the screen.

"Hi," Azem says.

His face ignites me. I struggle to push the way he makes me feel out of my mind.

"Hi." I pant.

"Were you still asleep?" Azem says.

"No, I'm awake. I was in the kitchen when you called." I yoga breath in through my nose, and release it.

"I understand." His gorgeous face lights up again. "I hope you don't mind me calling again." He says.

I walk back to the kitchen. "It's fine, I'm glad you called," I say.

"You're the first thing I thought about when I opened my eyes." He says.

Why is he doing this to me? "That's nice of you," I say.

"It's the truth." He corrects.

I prop the phone against the leg of a chair, then unravel the whole roll of paper towels to clean up the floor.

"What happened there?" He says.

"I knocked over a cup of coffee," I say.

"Zoe?" Azem asks.

I sit back on my knees as I stare at his face on the screen.

"What?"

"Have you changed your mind about having a boyfriend yet?"

I can't answer, so I pick the phone up and walk it over to the linen closet for the mop and Lysol.

We're both silent as I spray water and Lysol, on the floor, then glide the Swiffer over it until it's squeaky clean.

"I'm still waiting." Azem chants.

I prop the mop against the counter. I sit at the kitchen table and lean my phone against a bowl of glass fruit.

"I don't know if I've thought much more about it," I say.

He pinches his lips.

"Did you hear me?" I say.

"I'm trying to think of what I could say to make you say yes. You ask me." He suggests.

I crinkle my brow.

"It's an experiment, Zoe. Ask me to be your boyfriend."

I ask him.

"Yes," Azem says before I can finish asking.

"Why won't you say that to me?"

Azem is an anomaly. Everything about him reaches somewhere deep inside of me.

"Aren't there a school full of girls you still have to meet?" I say.

"What does that have to do with you?" He says.

"I'm saying I don't want you to regret your decision."

"Let me get this straight, you're telling me you want me to have options?"

I clench my temples with two fingers. "I'm saying, that I had fun last night, but nothing can happen with this. We're seniors, you know? I'm struggling.

"No, I don't know," Azem says.

"Aren't you going to college?" I counter.

"That has nothing to do with being your boyfriend." Azem is impossible to argue with.

"Azem, there's no point in starting something only to break up at the end of the summer." This is the first coherent thought I've had since this conversation began.

"I see your point." He says.

I exhale. He's finally ready to face reality.

"So you don't want to continue?" He confirms.

Panic paralyzes me. Azem's the kind of guy that doesn't play the gray area.

"I think we should focus on getting through senior year." My body feels a thousand pounds as the enormity of my words stands on my chest.

"You're right." He says.

No, I'm not right, please don't stop trying to make me your girlfriend. I give him a weak smile.

"I'll see you tomorrow morning." He says smiling that beautiful smile at me again.

"See you then."

V

By Monday, I miss Azem like a missing limb. Sunday night haunts me. All I want to hear is Azem asking me to be his girlfriend again. I want him to kiss me the moment I see him. Heaviness straddles my heart the whole ride to school.

When Azem and I meet up in the cafeteria, he smiles at me, but he feels a million miles away.

Standing on the outside of his affection is a lonely place. It's only the second day for him, and he is popular as hell. There must've been a cool kids meeting that inducted him into the popular club.

Everyone calls him Hanzem instead of Azem. Jessica and her lapdog cheerleaders fight for the chance of walking next to him while we walk down the hallway.

Lunch is even more unbearable. He doesn't care about whether I'm eating today. He's too busy entertaining a full table. Seeing that I'm no longer needed, I leave halfway through the lunch hour.

By the end of Azem's first full week of school, he's the most popular student. The only significant time I have with Azem is in Calculus III. Every time I sneak a peek over my shoulder he's concentrating on his work.

Before Thanksgiving break, Hendrat relieves me of my chaperoning duties.

"Thanks to you, Mr. Farak seems to be assimilating well. We appreciate you for being such a noble student for our foreign exchange program. Because of you, we'll see other students come in from all over the world." He says.

"You're welcome," I say, and jet out of his office.

With my life back in my own hands, I plunge into schoolwork. Studying has always been my crutch when life gets too overwhelming.

If I'm going to have any real chance of succeeding at Oxford, I have to stop thinking about Azem. If Oxford accepts me, it'll be my ticket to a new life. The fact that a dark theater and a slush is all it took to make me forget about my future is pathetic.

No sooner than my chaperoning ends, do rumors of which girl Azem is dating swirl. The thought of Azem taking another girl to the movies makes me sick to my stomach.

On Thanksgiving Eve, I come home after work, and there's a letter on my bed. A hot pink sticky note's attached to it.

"WHAT IS THIS?" The note from mom shouts.

When I notice the Oxford emblem I clamp my hand over my mouth. I've scoured the mailbox every day for the last month, trying to intercept this letter before she does. The one time she's actually home, it arrives. I put the letter in my panty drawer.

Raina was the person I turned to when I needed someone. Now, all she cares about is partying with her new friends.

With my mom pissed, and no one to help me face my letter from Oxford, I sink lower than I've been since my dad died.

That night, I fish around my mom's standing wardrobe closet. I push my arm all the way to the back and root and root around until I find an a bottle of wine. She knows that I've drunk it before, but she hides it anyway. For my mom, the illusion of having control is as good as the real thing.

I finish the bottle of Riesling in three glasses. I fill the bottle back up and pray that the leftover residue will flavor the water. It doesn't.

I plunge my hand into my mom's wardrobe again for looking for another bottle. I don't breathe until my hand grazes the cold hard glass of another bottle. The cork is impossible to get out. Any other time I hit my mom's stash I stop after a couple of glasses. When I finally get the hang of the corkscrew, there are pieces of cork floating at the top of the bottle. I switch out the cork from the previous bottle. I groan when I remember I have to drink another glass of wine to bring the bottle down to its original level.

Back in my room, I guzzle the glass of wine down like a shot. My mouth waters, so much that spit oozes out the corners of my mouth. I'm horrified at my pathetic reflection in the mirror. My eyeliner's smudged and my eyes are bloodshot. I'm reaching for a face towel to cleanse my face when I hear Azem's ringtone.

My heartbeat crawls and the four glasses of wine makes my head swirl. My mouth starts watering again. I cup my hand over my mouth, but vomit sprays through the cracks of my finger. I hunch over the toilet while my body lurches up everything in my stomach. Sharp pains wrack through my chest cavity with every violent convulsion. Vomit shoots out of my mouth in torrents that coat the inside of the toilet bowl and floor. My stomach muscles contract until nothing but bitter bile comes up.

I mash my eyes shut and flush the toilet. The bitter smells that waft out of the bowl make me sick all over again. Raina and her new friends always welcomed throwing up. She said it was the best medicine for too much alcohol. She always felt better after throwing up. All I want to do is burrow underneath my comforter until I'm normal again, whatever that is.

I hobble over to the linen closet. I spread towels over the vomit surrounding the toilet and wipe up my mess. I throw the towels away. I never want to see the towels again after tonight. I spray Lysol on the toilet bowl and floor, then wipe it until the horror show disappears. A hot shower I take feels like a gift after the mess I've made.

It isn't until I crawl back into bed that I remember about Azem's call. I almost call him back, but I can't pull off a conversation with him right now. My vanity feels like a mile away as I tiptoe over to it to get my phone.

There's a text from Azem. He wishes me a Happy Thanksgiving break.

Hot tears sail down my cheeks. My Thanksgivings will be anything but happy. My mom's schedule doesn't alter for holidays. She always works doubles the week of Thanksgiving. It's like she's trying to erase every part of her life that would make her think about pain. She's convinced herself that Thanksgiving isn't a big deal. We can cook food and eat any day she always says.

I volunteer to work extra days, but my supervisor urges me to go home and enjoy the time off. I hate myself for resorting to my mom's tactics for dealing with my own pain. In the morning, I search my fuzzy, hung over mind for a good reason to reach out to Azem. Then it dawns on me that I never responded back to his text. I was too busy trying to recover from my throw up fest.

Before I call Azem, I give myself the kind of makeover Raina would be proud of.

I text Happy Thanksgiving to Azem, then ask him if he wants to FaceTime.

He calls me immediately.

My sour stomach flips while I swipe to answer his FaceTime.

The minute I see his bright, handsome face, I cover my face and bawl like a toddler. I'm so embarrassed that I have to hang up.

When I'm calm again, I start over on my makeup. I've got to get out of this house. I don't know where I'm going, but I'm not staying here.

A half-hour later, I toss my letter from Oxford in my purse. I'm on the second to last step when the doorbell rings. I check the peephole and duck when I see Azem's elongated body. When he pounds on the door, I unlock and open up.

I open the door enough for a sliver of the cold winter air to pour in.

"Zoe, what's up?" Azem strains to get a better look at me.

"Sorry," I say in my fake telephone voice. "I'm fine." I open the door enough for him to see the pathetic smile on my face.

"You're not fine. Can I come in?" Azem says.

I step back to let him in. I lead him down the basement stairs to the couch.

"What's wrong Zoe?" Azem bends around me, to look in my eyes, but I can't look at him.

"Don't worry about earlier, it was nothing."

"You can't tell me not to worry about you."

I turn on him. "Well, you're wasting your time. As a matter of fact, you don't have to call me anymore."

Azem's forehead creases and I have to look away. "You're crying, and you want me to ignore it?"

I walk toward the steps and look up at the front door. The silence in the house is loud as Azem penetrates me with is coal black stare.

"If you want me to leave, I'll leave. Sorry I came." Azem stalks past me. He takes the stairs two at a time. His hand is on the doorknob when I break.

"I'm sorry. You haven't done anything wrong."

Azem doesn't turn around, but he removes his hand from the knob.

"You caught me at a bad time. I tried to pull myself out of it, but seeing you brought everything back." Exposing my deepest feelings is the most uncomfortable thing I've ever done.

Azem turns around and sits on the top step. He clasps his hands between his smoke gray joggers. "Where's your mom?"

"At work," I say.

"Can you talk to her when she's home?" I shake my head. She won't be home till Friday.

"You mean Thursday." He corrects.

"No, I mean Friday."

"But that's the day after Thanksgiving." Says Azem.

"I know. People don't take a day off from being sick." I say, hating how much I sound like my mother.

He hangs his head. "Zoe, why didn't you tell me?"

Silence.

"You could've called me." He says.

"We agreed to back off," I say.

Azem exhales. "No, I agreed to let you back away. Nothing has changed for me."

"I can't tell," I say.

"Zoe, I did what you wanted. What would you have had me do?"

He's right. I would've done the same thing.

"Will you come home with me for Thanksgiving?"

I shrug.

"Doesn't your mom want you to be happy for Thanksgiving? What will you eat?"

I don't have any answers.

"Pack a bag, so we can get out of here. Whatever we have to say or do to put your mom at ease we'll figure it out later."

I'm too hung over to fight. I walk up the stairs from the basement and look back down at him. He has his hair in one hand, closing his fist around it. He looks so worried about me that I almost start crying again.

It's quiet on the way Azem's house. All I've thought about is being close to him again.

"Did you?" Azem asks.

"What?" I say hating that my mind was so far away I didn't hear his question.

"Did you get everything that you need?" He repeats.

I scan my mind, then nod.

Satisfied, he turns back to the road.

"I hope you're not doing this because you feel sorry for me. You don't have to interrupt your plans like this." I say.

We're at a light and he stares at me while he shakes his head. A curl springs loose and he pushes it back. The light turns green, and he's still staring at me. The car behind us honks, and Azem drives, but he takes his time pulling off.

The silence in the car is strangling me. I want to fix whatever I messed up before we get out of the car. I can't stand so much friction between the two of us.

"Zoe, I mean everything I say to you. I wish you wouldn't doubt me so much."

Azem pulls into the driveway of a house so big, that it looks like he's pulling in to turn back around. When he pushes the button on the garage door holder clipped to his visor, I can't believe that this is his house.

Azem's garage can fit three cars, but we're the only car inside.

I'm glad I don't have to meet his mom right away. Especially since Azem and I are on such shaky ground.

"I'm sorry," I say.

"Don't apologize, Zoe. I want you to believe me when I say, that you're not keeping me from anything else." He reclines against his headrest.

I knead my temples. My throbbing headache is more ferocious than ever.

"Come on, so we can get something for your headache."

He picks my Gap duffel bag up off the back seat.

I get out of the car and follow him as he opens the door from the garage that leads inside his home.

I don't know what I was expecting Azem's house to be like, but the citrus smells and luxury that fills my senses wasn't it.

His house is modern, with floor space for days. His hallway is so long that I can do a full out sprint, and run out of breath before I run out of space.

The most striking thing about his house is the artwork. Beautiful pictures and motifs litter almost every wall and table. Azem says that his mom is an art glutton. They have to drag her out of art galleries. A picture that I fall in love with the moment I see is a woman with jet-black hair looking out over the desert. The wind has her hair sailing beside her, in a long silky black wave. The sky is cerulean without a single cloud. The desert sands are vast with rolling dunes that go on forever. The artist is so talented that to look at looking at the picture makes me feel like this woman. What she's thinking about as she looks out over the desert paradise, is everything on my mind.

I'm so mesmerized by the picture that Azem has enough time to put my bag away and get Tylenol for my headache.

"It's called "a'tqd", he says handing me a bottle of Fiji water and two white pills. I throw the pills to the back of my throat.

"Careful, it's already open." Azem nods at the blue top on the water bottle.

I down the pills, and return my focus back to the beautiful picture.

"It means "think." Azem's voice sounds like a song in the long hallway.

"I love it."

"Don't let my mom hear you say that, or she'll have you on art stakeouts with her." He warns.

"She's got great taste."

My stomach grumbles.

"When's the last time you ate?" Says Azem.

"Sometime yesterday at work."

Azem shakes his head. "Come on." He takes my hand and leads me through a maze to the kitchen. He parks me in a seat at the center island, then walks over to the refrigerator. He takes out some lettuce, tomatoes, and some sort of meat.

"Do you like roast beef?"

I nod.

He washes his hands at a matte silver swan-necked faucet. Copper pots dangle high in a glorious diagonal above my head.

Azem slices a tomato with his back to me, and a shiver runs up my spine. His jogging pants hang off his waist in such a sexy way.

Alone with him in this big beautiful house makes my nerve endings feel electric. Goosebumps break out on my arms when Azem walks two plates over. He folds a paper towel and saddles my plate with it. He doesn't touch his food until I eat first.

The roast beef is succulent and fatty. It tastes nothing like the gritty cuts my mom buys from the deli.

"Did your mom make this?"

Azem nods.

"She's a good cook." I wipe my mouth with the flower decorated paper towel.

"Thank you," Azem says.

"Where's your mom?"

"At the store shopping for Thanksgiving." He says.

The way his jaw flexes while he eats his sandwich makes me want to stop eating to watch him.

"She won't be back before tonight. She goes all out for any holiday." He pops the last corner of sandwich in his mouth.

After we eat, Azem washes our plates, dries them, and puts them back in the cabinets. Then, he takes me by the hand and leads me to the basement.

My hand feels so right clasped inside his. I wish I could keep his fingers threaded between mine al the time. He's the only person that makes me feel this warm and accepted.

I take in the basement area and marvel at how it's more like a condo. The bar, mini kitchen, huge flat screen, and endless shelving, is luxurious. The couch snakes around the basement.

There are several rooms in the basement, but I can tell by the grandeur of Azem's room that his is the master suite. There's no chance that he's brought any girls from school here. They would be stalking him right now. There are more than a few girls who stalk for a hobby.

"Want to watch a movie?" The corners of Azem's mouth curl.

I can't help smiling back. "Ok,"

We sit in the center of the couch. I don't know why, but I leave enough room between us to sit two people. Azem's busy fumbling with the Apple remote control to notice how much space there is. When he finds something satisfactory, he drops the remote into a compartment in the couch. He leans his body toward me.

My breath hitches.

"You look cold. Do you want a blanket?" He speaks into my ear, and I shiver.

I nod.

His lips graze my ear before he lifts up to get a blanket.

Azem brings the blanket back and coils up inside of it. He turns toward me after several beats. "What?" He says with a grin on his face.

"I thought the blanket was for me."

"It is." He turns back to the movie.

I scoot down the couch and unwrap the blanket that he has pinned to his body.

"Thank you," I say before I steal the blanket from him. I take it to my spot on the couch.

Azem crosses his arms over his chest. I like the way he's staring at me.

"May I share that with you?" His accent appears and it's intoxicating.

I move over to him and spread the blanket over the both of us.

"Thank you for everything." I have to stop talking when a lump gathers in my throat.

"Ana ahbk." Azem chants in my ear.

"Translation?" I say. I bite my lip waiting for his response.

"What does it feel like I said?" Azem says.

I can't answer him. I break his gaze to concentrate on the TV.

After a while, my eyelids won't stay open. When I wake up, I'm in Azem's bed.

My phone vibrates inside my purse. I root around until I find my phone. Despite my foggy vision, I see a zillion texts and missed calls from my mom. I text her that I'm at a friend's house and that I'm fine.

What friend? And don't say, Raina, because I already called her.

"I never said I was with her."

"Call me. NOW." She texts back.

I sit up straight in his bed. Despite the way my mom's pissing me off, I feel like royalty in this plush bed.

"Where are you?" She shouts when the call connects.

"I'm with a friend."

"You already told me that Zoe. Who is this friend?" My mom says.

"Azem." I almost call her Claire, but I know better. A low battery banner flashes on the screen of my phone. "You're with the foreign exchange student?" She spits out.

"Yes," I admit.

"Are you dating this boy now?" She grills.

I hate that I don't know the answer to her question.

"Mom, I'm here with him because he's concerned about me."

"Concerned about what?" She yells.

"That I'll have to spend Thanksgiving alone."

"Honey, you know that people don't take a day off from being sick. Someone has to be here." My mom preaches.

I roll my eyes. "I know mom. That's why I'm here."

She sighs. "I've got to get back to my station, but we've got some things to talk about later. And I want you home when I call you back. Do you understand?"

"I'm not going home tonight mom."

"Zoe Alina Mason." I almost laugh at her pathetic assertion of authority. "Why should I have to go home and be by myself for Thanksgiving?"

"That's not the point Zoe. It's this guy you're with. He may have left his old country, but trust me, he will always believe a certain way, and they do not treat women well. I am not allowing you to be under his influence. Next thing you know you'll be wrapped up from head to toe."

"Mom, you don't know anything about him." I bite down my anger.

"I know enough to forbid you from going anywhere near him outside of your chaperoning at school. As a matter of fact, I'll call your school and have them elect someone else as his chaperone."

"Mom." I try to protest, but she cuts me off.

"Look, I can't talk about this right now. Go home and we'll talk about it later."

She ends our call, and the silence in his room smothers me. I can't imagine what has her so worked up about Azem. She doesn't care about anything that I do, as long as I make good grades. For her to forbid me from seeing Azem is crazy. We're not dating for one, and even if we are, he's not anything like the monster she's making him out to be. He rejects everything about his former home. From what he's told me, he never agreed with the laws of his homeland. Even as a child, he knew that something was horribly wrong. It's insulting for my mom to think I'm stupid enough to allow a guy to brainwash me. Knowing how irrational she is about Azem makes me want to date him just to piss her off.

I climb out of bed and search for my shoes. My black graffiti print Nikes sit neatly underneath the bed.

Azem isn't on the couch. I'm afraid to call out for him, for fear that his mom will discover me, and throw me out in the cold.

I creep up the basement steps Panic sets in when I get to the top. I can't find my way back to the kitchen. I call Azem. "Where are you?" I whisper. Another low battery notification pops up on my phone's home screen. My charger is the one thing I forgot to pack.

Azem appears out of nowhere. He looks amused that I'm lost in his house. Hand in hand he directs me back to the kitchen.

Familiar spices flood my sense of smell as soon as we enter the kitchen. He parks me at the island again, then takes his position at the stove. This time he's pushing something around in a copper pan.

"I hope you like Hamburger Helper." He looks over his shoulder for my confirmation.

"Who doesn't like Hamburger Helper?" I say.

"I'd never heard of it until a month ago," Azem says.

Azem speaks English so well that I forget that he's from a completely different world. He's so refined that it's hard to imagine him dwelling in the desert. "Does your family eat it a lot?" Azem asks.

I'm glad that he turns back around to the pan after he asks me this. If it wasn't for Hamburger Helper I would have gone hungry when dad died. I thought I was a real chef when I figured out how to prepare the one skillet meal. "Yeah, we ate it a lot especially after my dad." I have to stop.

Azem adds all the packets, milk and water to the pan, then turns the heat down. Azem comes over to me and takes my hand. "I'm sorry about your dad."

He isn't the first person to tell me that, but he is the first person that I believe.

"Did you talk to your mom?" He says.

"You could call it that." I kneed my temples with my middle finger and thumb. My headache thrashes around like a tsunami. "May I have more Tylenol?"

"I'll be right back." Azem disappears from the kitchen. He stops at the refrigerator for a bottle of water, then brings the medication to me. He shakes out two pills and opens the water for me.

"Thank you," I say.

"You're welcome." He says on his way back over to the skillet.

I rub the cold bottle of Fiji over my forehead as I watch him stir the food.

He adjusts the heat on the stove again, then replaces the top. "What'd she say?" He says when he's back from the stove. He pulls the bottle away from my hand and sits it on the counter.

I tell him our conversation, minus her crazy assumptions about his motives. Azem doesn't interrupt once.

"She'd have a valid reason to be nervous if I wasn't Christian now."

"I told her she had nothing to worry about, but she's too stubborn," I say.

"That's one of the reasons why it's so hard for me to get through to my brothers and father. There's a lifetime of lies to chip away at. No sooner do you chip a lie off, does another lie grow in its place 10 times stronger."

I can tell that reaching his father and siblings is the one true desire of his heart. My heart breaks as I imagine that if it was going to happen, they would already be here with him.

"So, what are you going to do?" He says breaking out of his thoughts.

"I'm not going home," I say.

He smiles. "Good, because if your mom's going to hate me, I want her to have a good reason."

"She doesn't hate you," I say.

"With all due respect, I'm not focused on how she feels. I only about your opinion." Says Azem.

His eyes are dissolving me.

He leaps up off the high-backed stool and hightails it to the stove. He yanks the top off the pot, and steam hits him square in the face. Azem jerks his head back and fans the steam away.

It's impossible to be around Azem and concentrate on anything else. The food is delicious, but it's nothing compared to him.

He wasn't lying when he said his mom would be out all day. The darkening sky casts comforting shadows through the French doors in the kitchen.

"Do you want some tea, or something a little stronger?" Azem snickers.

My stomach does a three-sixty degree flip. I shake my head slowly.

"I'm still trying to recover. That's why didn't respond back to you last night." I say.

"I figured. Can't hold your liquor?" Azem teases.

It hurts to laugh. "It usually doesn't affect me like this." I pause. "I was in a crazy space last night. I got a letter from Oxford yesterday."

"London, huh?" Azem's almond-shaped eyes penetrate mine. His lashes are enviable.

"It's my number one choice. My mom shuts down any conversation about going to school in London. She found the letter yesterday."

Azem takes my empty plate and stacks it on top of his. Then he walks it to the sink. He comes back with a dishtowel and wipes the counter.

"Your mom's afraid of you leaving her alone."

I can't stand to hear Azem tell me the truth about her. He folds the dishrag up as far as it'll go and launches it from his seat to the sink.

"Did you get in?" Azem says.

I shrug. "I was too afraid to open it."

"We can go back to your house, and you can open it with me if you want to."

I pull him up off his stool by his hand. "We don't have to go that far."

We face each other Indian style on his bed. I clutch the letter to my chest. I smell the envelope and run my fingers over the embossed symbols on the front.

"Would you open the letter already?" Azem laughs.

"I can't."

"Here, give it to me." He urges.

I hand him the letter and then snatch it back.

He steals it from me and turns around and peels the envelope open.

I try to reach around him, but the more I touch his broad shoulders the weaker I get.

Azem has the envelope open, and he slips the tri-folded letter out.

I leap off the bed and pace the floor. Before long, I'm peeking over his shoulders again. He smells like soap and masculinity. Even his hair has a distinct cocoa fragrance that makes me want to close my eyes and inhale him.

"Clearing Offer, Thank you for your Clearing inquiry. I am happy to tell you that we are able to offer you a place on the following degree program: BA: English and History." Azem's British accent is awful, but the words that he says can't be more beautiful coming off his tongue.

I sit back on my heels and bury my face in the palms of my hands.

"You did it," Azem says attempting to peel my hands away.

I allow him to loosen my hands, then I wrap my arms around his neck.

He hugs me, with every inch of his body. My excitement over my acceptance letter from Oxford disappears. As soon as his body makes full contact with mine nothing else matters. As scintillating as it was to kiss him at the movies, this is so much more. Azem is what I want. As ecstatic as I am about Oxford, I'm happier to be here with him, like this. The muscles in his arms contract as he holds me tighter. His hands travel down my body until his hands slip into the back pockets of my jeans. It's the sexiest thing. My stomach clenches as he kisses the crown of my head. A woman sings out his name before I can reach up to kiss him back.

We climb off his bed. I reach for my tennis shoes. "Leave those." He says.

I put them on anyway.

He bends down to his knees in front of me and unlaces my shoes.

"Azem, I can't meet your mom barefooted."

He pulls one shoe off, then unlaces and slips the other shoe off. "My mom isn't stuck up Zoe, she's going to love you."

"How do you know? Because I love you." Azem stands back up and his tall, muscular figure looms over me. I swallow my tears back down and follow him upstairs.

We find his mom in the kitchen.

"Aaah, there you are my handsome." She says it like a nursery rhyme. She freezes when her eyes settle on me. She takes my hand, spins me around then hugs me. She smells like very expensive perfume.

"Zoe, it's so good to finally be able to set my sights on you." She says.

Her voice is melodic, like every sentence she says is a lyric in a song.

"May I?" She holds her hand out. I don't know what she's talking about, but she's so nice that I say yes. She runs a hand over my hair. "Zoe, you're more beautiful than Azem describes you."

"Ok, mom," Azem says pulling me back toward him. I love the way they fight over me.

His mom smiles at Azem then winks at me. We follow her over to the kitchen table.

"I told you." He mouths and flashes a lethal smile. I can't wait to be alone with him again, especially with the L-bomb he dropped on me.

A tall bald man with skin the color of dark chocolate sits at the long banquet table. He stands up as we approach. He takes my hand inside his massive hand and we shake.

"Hello, Zoe." His voice is deep and commanding. He would be intimidating if he wasn't so pleasant.

"This is Roger." His mother says.

"Nice to meet you," I say.

Azem and Roger give each other a full hug, and I can tell they genuinely like each other. I've got a million questions, but I don't know where to start.

"Thank you, son, for cooking. We've been shopping all day and I'm starved."

She scoops out two portions of Hamburger Helper onto a plate for Roger, and one for herself.

"Mom, guess which picture Zoe likes?"

She replaces the top on the skillet, places the plate on the counter and spins on her heels. Her waist length hair whips around her.

"Which one?" She looks like she's holding her breath waiting for my answer.

"Think," I say.

She claps her hands and looks at Roger. "That'll be five dollars, sir." She delivers the plates to the table.

He clasps a five between his fingers. He kisses her cheek and she smiles up at him.

"We have a standing bet that every guest who visits will like Think. It's the only way he would allow me buy it." She laughs, and Roger's deep chuckle follows.

"Thank you so much, Zoe," Roger says.

"Sorry," I say.

"Don't mention it. I'm glad that Zara's got a new art partner." Roger says relieved.

I look at Azem. "I told you he whispers."

They eat and Azem and I fill them in on school. It hurts to talk about school since we haven't been on speaking terms.

My news about Oxford impresses Roger and Zara. The two of them look at me with approval.

"I'm sure you two have plenty to celebrate about. Please excuse us so that Roger and I can beautify the house. We'll call you up when we're finished." Zara says.

Roger clears his throat. "What she meant to say is excuse us so that Roger can beautify the house." Says Roger.

"That's what I said." Zara winks at me and smiles a dazzling white smile.

"Off you go," Zara says, then swats Azem on the butt.

We go back downstairs.

We huddle under the blanket and watch TV while his mom and Roger decorate the house.

Hours later, Zara texts us back upstairs. The house is breathtaking. Each centerpiece and decoration is clever and inviting. The heart of the decorations is in the kitchen. Golden plates and gold utensils gleam around the table. Large bejeweled gold goblets stand at each setting. Champagne colored runners shimmer down the table. Rich burgundy curtains adorn the floor to ceiling windows.

For such a small woman, Zara's taste is gigantic. She doesn't miss any details. Everything down to the gold napkin holders looks well thought out. It's hard to place Zara in the Middle East. The regal way she carries herself couldn't have come from such oppression.

"You're such a good decorator," I say.

"Thank you." Both Roger and Zara reply. She pinches Roger's cheek then stands on her tip-toes to kiss him.

"Thank you, love, for helping me so much." She says.

"You're welcome." Roger bends down and kisses her.

Azem pulls me away from the kitchen.

When the smells of Thanksgiving pour into the basement, I miss my mom.

The lock screen on my phone is full of missed calls from her. As much as I wish I could have a normal conversation with her, I know she's in no mood to be nice. I swipe the notifications away, pretending that by doing so, I can forget about her.

"Ready to go to bed?" Azem says.

My stomach flips over. "Yeah," I say, hoping I don't sound as excited as I am.

"You can borrow anything you need if you don't have anything to sleep in." Azem peels his sweatshirt and t-shirt over his head at the same time. His eyes pin me in place.

"Or if you prefer to sleep naked, that's cool too."

Azem's jeans are halfway down as he says this.

"No, I've got something. Thanks." I fish around my duffle bag for my Pink shirt gown.

When I come out of Azem's bathroom, he's already in bed. It's not until I slip inside his comforter that I confirm that he's not a naked sleeper. I let my exhale out in short, controlled breaths.

"Can you do something for me?" His upper body muscles elongate as he reaches for the cord on his lamp. "Will you wear that gown every time you spend the night?" His smile ignites me.

I'm glad he turned the lights out before he could see how wide my smile is.

"Come here." The weight shifts in the bed, as Azem, leans over me and scoops me over to him until I'm against his chest.

"How am I can I kiss you all the way over there?"

I can hear his smile.

"How do you know I want you to kiss me?" I say around a yawn that I can't hold in.

"That's true." Azem starts pushing me back over to my side, but I hook one leg around his waist.

"I said how do you know, not that I didn't want to," I say.

Azem pulls me up until I can feel his breath on my lips. "Kiss me, Zoe." His lips graze mine with each word he says.

I kiss his eyelids, and he exhales a deep groan that makes me shiver. I make a path down his face until I finally get to his lips. "You're right, I want you to kiss me," I say against his lips without kissing him.

His fingers dance down my neck then he bites down on my lower lip. His nibbling feels so good. When his lips pull on mine, my mind blurs. It takes a while for me to regain my bearings when he stops.

"Get some sleep," Azem says.

"Good night," I settle against his hard chest.

A heavy fatigue settles over me. Before I fall asleep I try to think of a way I can let him know that the next time I don't want him to stop.

Azem's mom cooks enough food for the four of us to eat for a week. Exotic Middle Eastern dishes and American dishes share the table. Ahem has to tell me the names of the succulent foreign dishes.

After several plates of food, Azem and I join Zara and Roger in the upstairs den. The soft lighting and stuffed stomachs paralyze us all. When faking interest in the Hallmark movies exhausts Azem, he takes my hand to go back downstairs. He bends over the leather couch to kiss his mother's cheek. Azem thumps the back of Roger's head, and we hightail it out of the den.

Back downstairs, the excitement of being alone wakes us both up.

I can sense Azem's reserve as he kisses a trail down my neck. He stops before he reaches my breasts. My nerves won't give me permission to tell him that I want more. I wish he could read my mind, or better yet smell the pheromones I'm giving off. If we were animals this would be so much easier. I wouldn't have to come up with the courage to tell him that I want him to pull my shirt over my head. Those invisible signals would alert him that I want him to unhook my bra, and touch my breasts all he wants. He would automatically know to strip me until I'm naked. I scrape my mind off the floor of the gutter for a moment to regain some semblance of self-control. My imagination forgets that I've never actually had sex before.

When Azem pulls back up to hunker down in the covers beside me, my body confirms that it would know what to do with him.

Going there with a guy at Easton is a one-way ticket to whoredom. Everyone knows that a whore brand in high school follows you for the rest of your life. The college guys that Raina tried to hook me up with weren't any better, but at least we didn't have to go to the same school.

Every time Azem's full and firm, but somehow soft lips touch my skin, there isn't any room for fear. Instead of fear, there's a base arousal that makes me want to fist his hair with both hands until he can't miss that I want him.

He kisses me again. I still don't have the nerve to tell him what I want, but I'm determined to show him. I'm so excited as his tongue darts in and out of my mouth that I trash the hair grabbing idea. I'm liable to yank too hard and ruin the mood. Instead, I lift up when he pulls away. The ridge of his neck is warmer than usual as my tongue traces a long, steady line all the way up the rim of his ear. When I lay back down, I feel his upper body shudder over me. He sweeps his thumb down my cupid's bow until he softly pinches my lower lip between his fingers.

"Are you sure?" Azem says while he pokes his pelvis seductively against me. His head dives into my shoulder blade when I guide his fingers to the slick spot between my thighs.

With a surgeon's precision, Azem pulls my gown up over my head. He does mountain climbers out of his shorts. He feasts on my neck, inching ever closer to the point that he always stops. When he crosses his self-imposed threshold my mind implodes. He takes his time exploring my breasts in a manner that is both reverent and ferocious. The strength behind every pull his lips take of my breasts and nipples makes me arch off the bed. Each time my body lifts, his lips are there to catch me. His hand splays on my stomach, as he guides me back down on the bed. When he travels down to the money spot, I can't prepare myself for the sensation. What he's doing to me makes me unravel. I grasp for a pillow to cover my face, but Azem's strong hand pulls it away and flings it across the room.

"Only you and I can hear." He groans.

My legs start shaking as soon as he says this. He takes his time licking and stroking me with his tongue. A flood of pulsations, make time and space drift away from my consciousness. My mind floats away from the room for an indefinable time. When I come back to my senses, I can taste my body on his lips.

I shiver while he slides a condom over his penis. I can't see anything in the pitch-black room, but I don't need sight to feel how big he is. I cram my eyes closed when he tunnels inside me. I wait for excruciating pain that never comes. Azem feels so good plunging in and out of me. The sounds we make are less than dignified, but it doesn't matter. He gobbles my lips in his mouth. I pant into his ear, and he whispers into mine. We trade undignified sounds into each other's ears, and mouths. It feels so natural to do this with him, that I can't congratulate myself for finally exiting the V club. Sex with anybody else wouldn't have been this good.

After round one, he cleans me off.

When I'm settled against his chest again. Painful tears well up in my eyes. I don't know why any of this with Azem is happening to me, but I never want it to stop.

He caresses me, while our heartbeats return to resting.

"That was my first time going all the way," I confess.

"Mine too." Says Azem.

I spring up to look him in the eyes if I could see him. "What?" He says.

"You're so good," I say.

He pulls me up until our lips touch. "That's because you're so good." He licks my lips, and a shiver runs down the length of my body.

"You can't do stuff like that anymore," I say.

"Why not?" Azem sounds concerned.

"Because it's too tempting now," I say.

He licks me again. "Sounds good to me." He jerks away from my lips before I can kiss him.

"You're on towel duty next," Azem says, then wraps one arm around my back, and flips me over on my stomach.

It's impossible to get out of bed when you're sharing it with Azem. He's even sexier in the morning. His gruff, scratchy voice makes it impossible for me to resist him. It's also impossible to get clean when you have sex during the shower, and after the shower is over.

I'm too nervous to face his mom again. What Azem did to me all night, and half the morning is plain on my face. Azem assures me that she wants him to have the privacy to live his own life. She never violates his personal space. When she needs something, she texts him.

I glance at my phone while I get dressed. I wish I could have this kind of peace for the rest of my life. I am not in the mood to face my mom, especially after our last conversation. She has to know that I haven't been home. I already know she's pissed.

"Will you have brunch with me before I take you home?" Azem says cradling me from behind. I could cry like a preschooler right now. He looks so handsome, the way his damp hair falls over his forehead.

"I wish I didn't have to go." I close my eyes as tears spill over the edges. He brushes my tears away, then hugs me tight against him. I love it when he traps me in his arms. I've needed to feel this strength for a long time. It's hard to think about going back to my cold, bitter world.

"I don't want you to leave either." He nestles his lips into the crook of my neck. I turn around and hug him back. He picks me up off my feet, I wrap my legs around his waist, and he carries me back to his bed.

We never make it upstairs for brunch, instead, we say goodbye.

VI

Mom's talking to someone in the kitchen when I get home. I can't close the door to my bedroom and get in bed fast enough.

Ten minutes later she helps herself into my room.

"How was your Thanksgiving?" Mom says.

"It was ok."

I'm in love.

"You got plenty to eat?" She says.

I can't get enough of him.

I nod.

"You didn't think to bring your old mom a plate?"

Got me.

"It's ok, we had a potluck." She waves me off. Before she closes the door she adds, "Zoe, I realize you are a senior, but you are still very much a child. My child."

I'm a woman now, mom, and nothing you say can change that.

"I'm too tired to talk about how you disobeyed me. So, all I'll say is the next time I tell you to do something, you better do it. Do you understand?"

I nod at her delusions.

"Alright. There's frozen pizza in there for dinner tonight." She closes the door behind her.

I kick my comforter off. I'm so sick of her. I wish I could tell her the truth about who she is. She would rather that I spend Thanksgiving scared in this fucking house. Azem's family actually cares about me. They fed me real food on Thanksgiving, not the frozen trash she leaves behind for me every day.

My mom acts like she's the sole proprietor of grief. People die. Dad's gone, and I hate it, but what about me? Why can't I have a mom, because she can't have her husband? I can't go and marry another mother. If I could it would be Zara.

Even with a hole in her heart big enough to fit eleven children, she's still the most winsome person I've ever met. She has even more of a reason to abuse depression, but she doesn't take it out on Azem.

I close my eyes and push everything out except him. I'm supposed to be celebrating finally having sex. He could not have felt better. Sex with him is like eating your favorite dish, except each bite tastes better than the first.

My mom's voice rouses me out of sleep, She's on her way to work again. For one of the first times, I'm not upset that she's gone, I'm happy, because I get to FaceTime Azem all night long.

Sitting in the lover's corner at lunch isn't so awkward now, especially since we're actually together now.

It takes two weeks for the stragglers to catch on that we want to eat alone. When the most persistent hangers-on keep pulling up a chair, we pull out our Calculus III books. Calculus scares them off so good that we hate we didn't try it earlier.

Going to Azem's house every day after school becomes my daily goal. It's a miracle that we ever make it out of his car. The issue of birth control nags at me every time the condom breaks. I hate the idea of taking a pill every day. A research paper I did last year changed my mind about the so-called harmless little pill. The overproduction of Estrogen causes side effects that I refuse to subject my body to.

Azem kisses me, then scales the bed. He walks bowlegged to the bathroom.

I follow him and hop in the shower with him.

I help him change the sheets on his bed. I tuck my side of the sheets underneath his mattress and freeze.

Tears sting my eyes.

Azem notices a tear falling off the tip of my nose.

"What's wrong? Did I hurt you?" He rushes to my corner of the bed and pulls me onto his lap.

I throw my arms around his neck.

"Come on, tell me." He squeezes me.

"I'm so sorry." I whimper.

"Zoe, help me out here."

I shake my head.

"You told me you loved me on Thanksgiving and I completely ignored you. I'm so sorry, I meant to say it back. I love you too, so much." I yammer.

Azem tries to pry me away from his neck, but I can't face him.

"Zoe, I know you love me."

I face him.

"It's not ok, for me to leave you hanging like that." I persist.

Azem stares at me for a long time.

"Zoe, if my love for you depended on your love for me, then it wouldn't be real." He explains.

"I love you so much," I say.

He kisses me.

"I know you do," Azem says.

He pulls me back on the bed and wraps us in his comforter.

"How do you feel about birth control?" I ask.

Azem shrugs.

"I support it if that's what you're asking." He says.

I lift up on one elbow.

"I support the theory, of being careful, but I can't justify taking medication that does more harm than good," I explain.

Azem strokes my face with a thumb.

"The choice is yours." He says.

I lay back down, more confused than ever.

For him to trust my instincts is almost worse than having an opinion on the matter. It's not like I would let him forbid me from taking it, or anything. It's more like, I trust us more than a synthetic drug.

"Are you getting some?" He asks.

"I don't think so," I confess.

"Why not?" Says Azem.

"Because we have more control over our sex lives than a pill." I decide.

"I agree." He says with a glint in his eyes.

Despite my mom's resistance to me spending time anywhere else but home, she's still working like a mad woman. For the first time in six years, I'm glad to have so much time alone. More time alone means more time with Azem.

The week of Christmas mom's hospital had a family admitted with full body, third-degree burns. Their tragic story was all over the news. The fire department said that the smoke alarms in their house were under recall. The family never had their units replaced. The mother, boyfriend, and seven-year-old daughter had survived. The seven-week-old baby girl was dead on arrival.

My mom oozed with pride while she blathered on about how her boss only trusted her to care for them.   Her head inflated to blimp proportions the more she bragged.

I struggled to keep my eggs down the longer she told her story.

I should call the hospital to inform them that her own daughter is on life support.

In years past, I had frozen dinners and boxed cakes to look forward to for Christmas. This year, I could hardly tamp down my excitement when I bid her goodbye before she went to the hospital.

Not only do Azem, Zara, and Roger want me to spend Christmas with them, they expected it.

Azem picked me up two days before Christmas. With my mom at work all night, I had a chance to do all the normal things every other family does to prepare for the holiday.

We race to his house. The idiot behind us is in the same hurry, the way he's riding Azem all the way to the Barrows.

"That asshole better be glad you're in here with me."

A vein in Azem's temple pops out. I've never seen him so angry. Even anger looks good on him.

I lean over and kiss his ear. "Is there anything I can do to help you relax?"

He immediately loosens his grip on the steering wheel and turns his face toward me. His lips brush mine, as he speaks. "I don't know, it has to be pretty relaxing." He insists.

"My mom won't belong." He says as we take turns peeling each other's clothes off on the steps to the basement.

I nod my head as we struggle to kiss, without falling down the steps. Somehow we make it to his bed without any major injuries.

Azem reaches over to the top drawer of his nightstand for a Magnum.

I bite the condom out of his mouth and spit it on the bed.

"You've never put it inside anyone have you?"

"No, Zoe," Azem huffs. He bends down to kiss me again.

My fingers push against his chest, and he lifts up.

"Even in Jerusalem?" I grill.

His thick hair springs over his brow as he dips his head. He hops out of bed. "I hear my mom." He picks up his boxer briefs off the floor and hops into them. He hurries out the room for the rest of his scattered clothes before I can process what I've done.

I creep after him. I dress as I go. When I make it upstairs, Roger, Zara, and Azem are standing over a huge bowl of gold popcorn.

"Hi, my letter sake." She winks at me and smiles Azem's smile.

My heart swells at her greeting but deflates when I notice how Azem's avoiding direct eye contact with me.

I'm in no mood for Christmas cheer, but I can't afford to lose the affection of Azem's family, even if I'm losing his.

"Come see." She waves me over to a huge bowl. She reminds me of Princess Jasmine with her long loose braid slung over her shoulder. I join the trio at the bowl.

"This is golden corn, and we're going to string tinsel, like in the old days. It's completely edible. The gold is food coloring," she explains.

I eye one puff up close. It smells so delicious and buttery, that my mouth waters.

"But no eating." She warns.

I drop the puff back into the bowl. She hands each of us a long piece of golden string with a golden needle threaded through the eye.

It's impossible to concentrate on stringing tinsel when Azem's in the same room. He keeps biting his lower lip while he strings.

I'm so turned on, that my stomach cramps.

We string fast, especially since Zara has several strings of popcorn finished.

"Ok, let's start stringing the tree so we can see how much we have to go." Zara sings.

We walk our strings of popcorn to her golden ornamented tree. Even the tips of the pine needles sparkle gold. Zara has a serious hang up with gold. I'll have to remember to ask Azem about it if he ever talks to me again.

I string as high as I can go, which isn't very high since I'm barely five foot three inches. I'm on my tiptoes with my last piece of string, when warmth covers me.

Azem takes my string and places it in the spot I'm aiming for. I am good for nothing while his tight torso and pelvis press in on me.

He whispers in my ear, "You're my first and last." He kisses my ear.

My heart fills back up and threatens to burst.

Now that the tree is strung, Zara may allow us to escape back downstairs.

This time the only sounds that will come from my mouth will be in a language that only Azem and I speak.

I announce that I'm going downstairs to get my phone. On the way downstairs, I pray that Azem follows me.

I undress and get under the covers. The sheets are cold, but I don't shiver until Azem slips inside the room, and locks the door behind him.

On Christmas Eve, Zara and Roger finish up their Christmas shopping. Azem and I finish nothing. Instead, we have sex over and over again.

A spicy aroma tempts us out of Azem's bed that evening. A huge pot of vegetable stew simmers in a tall stockpot. It's as rich and savory as any stew I've ever had. Carrots, celery, onions, leeks, turnips, a host of spices, and thick brown gravy make her stew my favorite.

I ask Zara about the delicious dish.

Zara recants how she cooked this stew at the end of every month. She had to be strategic about it because she was celebrating Christmas. If she anyone would have found out, she would've been in grave danger. She nicknamed it her child chow since she has twelve children. Her voice shakes. She looks like she's staring at a page from her past.

I imagine that she's looking right into each one of her children's faces.

Her long hair waves us goodbye as she hurries out of the kitchen.

I search Azem's face.

Azem picks up my hand. He's already covering it with his own. He kisses my knuckles.

"It's ok, she'll be fine. Be right back." He kisses my cheek and leaves behind a sliver of stew.

I wipe at my face with one hand.

Roger and I are alone.

He smiles at me. "Zara misses her children. That's all. You didn't do anything wrong." Says Roger.

"Have you ever met them?"

He shakes his head. "As many pictures as I've seen, and the way she talks about them, it's like I know them, but no, they don't know I exist."

I can't help but catch the sorrow of her situation.

"It's best this way." He says, reassuring me again.

I'm not hungry anymore. I want to go to Zara and tell her that I'm sorry for everything she's going through.

Azem comes back in the kitchen and takes his seat. He digs back into his bowl of stew.

"Can I go talk to her?" I say.

He halts the spoonful aimed at his mouth and takes my hand instead.

Azem knocks on her door, and her pleasant voice rings out to come in.

When he pushes her doors open the first word that comes to my mind is imperial.

Her room, not surprising is gold. Unlike the gold in other parts of the house, this gold looks like it takes eons to polish.

I'm scared to touch anything.

She's sitting on a gold, tiger clawed vanity bench. The pillowed bench top is so soft, that her petite body sinks down in the middle.

The only sounds in her room are that of the boar's bristles gliding down her black hair.

When she notices me standing beside Azem, she shoos him out and walks me back over to her vanity bench.

We sit.

She continues where she left off, brushing her coal black hair. After several strokes, she turns to me.

She places her brush in some sort of brush-shaped gold dish.

"This feels like the right time. Yes?" Zara asks.

I nod like a goof.

When she stands up, I glance in the mirror and hurry to lick the dried stew away before she turns back around.

Zara's holds a large rectangular thing. It's wrapped in beautiful gold wrapping paper. She holds it out toward me.

"For you." She says.

I don't move.

She has to wave me over to her.

I tear at the gold wrapping paper. My pace speeds up the more I expose. I can't believe what this is. "Think," I say and stare open mouthed at her. "Zara, I can't take this," I argue.

"And why can you not?" Zara demands.

"This is your painting. I can't."

"False, you can take it, and you will take it." Her judgment is final.

"But why?" I help her move it against her footboard.

Her bed looks like it belongs in a palace.

"Because I staked so much of my thoughts of beauty on long flowing hair until I saw you. I have never seen a woman look more beautiful. Forgive me if I offend, but it's your lack of hair that makes you so beautiful. You completely changed my mind." Zara finishes.

I back up to the vanity, and glance at my reflection when I sit down. I don't see any of what she's talking about. My self-esteem is fine, but the person she's describing isn't me.

"I confess that when Azem came home stumbling over his own tongue about you, I thought he was crazy. Oh, mom, you've got to see her. She's the most beautiful girl you've ever seen. And the thing is she has no hair. You're all he's been talking about since the first day of school." Zara smiles at my reflection in the vanity.

I'm both flattered and perplexed.

"I didn't know what to expect. When I saw your beautiful cheekbones, lovely brown hair, and slanted dark cat eyes, I understood." She admits.

She is drowning me. "Thank you, Zara. I don't know what to say."

"You've already said it." She says.

We stand up.

I almost forget the reason I came here in the first place. I didn't come here for her to make me feel better.

"I'm sorry about your children," I offer.

"No apologies from you Zoe. You're not the cause of my heartbreak."

We reach the door, and she hugs me. It's the kind of hug my mom never gives me.

We walk back to the kitchen together.

She latches on to Roger's massive upper arm beside him at the kitchen table. She nods her head when his deep voice questions her.

I look around for Azem. When I finally spot him, he's holding a finger to his lips before he crooks his pointer finger toward him. I almost leap off my stool, but I play it cool.

"She gave me."

"Think." Azem finishes for me.

"How did you know?"

"I had a clue when it disappeared off the wall." His lips capture mine before I lay back down on his chest.

It's embarrassing that I didn't notice the picture was gone from the wall. It can't be a good thing for Zara to gift me her favorite painting since I forgot all about it.

I swipe my tongue across his pebbled nipple. His torso flexes, and I trace each of his hard abs with my tongue.

Soon we're flinging sheets, pillows, and limbs off the bed.

When the last twist of his hips pushes against me, he slumps down on my chest.

"Sorry." Azem tries to roll over, but I pin him against me.

"I love it," I say, pulling him closer to me.

He pushes up and shelves my face between his long fingers.

"I love you, Zoe. I don't care how young we are. You're my life."

My throat constricts. "I love you too Azem."

I can feel his hardness pressing against my belly button.

"Merry Christmas." He pulls a box from underneath the only remaining pillow on the bed. He opens the velvet box and tilts the ring so I can get a good look. There's a tiny light showcasing the simple, yet stunning ring.

My nipples knot up as coolness replaces Azem's strong torso.

He's on the floor.

"You are the first, the last and the only woman I'll ever love. As rough as life was back home, I would go through it ten times, if it meant you were waiting for me on the other side. You're all I care about in this world. Will you be with me, as my wife Zoe?

Azem is pleading with me as if I could possibly say no.

"Azem how will we get married?"

Azem pops up on the balls of his feet. "You have to say yes before you can start worrying." He kisses the tip of my nose, then resumes kneeling.

"Yes." I pull him back up on the bed.

He brings the comforter and another pillow back up with him.

"How, Azem?" I listen to his thumping heartbeat. His deep voice calms me down.

"We'll do it when the time is right. And not in twenty years. We'll do it when we can make decisions independent of our parents."

"What if your mom disagrees with this?" I say.

Azem lifts my chin so that he has my attention.

"She won't. But to answer your hypothetical question, this is my decision to make alone. She nor anyone else has a part in it." He draws me in for the kisses that I never want to live without again.

"I understand that you can't wear your ring, so will you do something for me?" Azem says.

I hold my breath for his request.

"Will you accept that I don't lie to you, Zoe? Will you trust that I will always protect you in every way? There's no one above you nor will there ever be. Please say you will accept these things."

"I accept." I straddle him and pull him up until we're hugging chest to chest. I don't hold back this time when my tears threaten to fall. For the first time in my life, my guard is completely down.

Another hour of thrashing around his bed squeezes us dry. He holds me from behind with one arm scooping me into his body. His tight bicep and forearm curled around my middle make me feel so safe.

I wear my ring while we have sex, but right after I put it in the top drawer of his nightstand. We can't afford to misstep now. Not when he only has two months until he's eighteen and I have four. As nice as the solitaire princess cut diamond ring is, it's dull compared to the love he ignites inside of me. As long as I have him, I don't need anything else.

Vibrations buzz against the nightstand.

I push my hips back into Azem's pelvis. "Azem." I groan.

I nudge him again.

His pelvis pokes me back.

I turn over when his head slumps behind my mine after a while.

"Wake up. Your phone." I say trying to kiss him awake.

He kisses me ferociously.

"Azem, get the phone." I pant.

Azem pulls away from my lips but commands me to stay put.

My stomach tingles as I wait for him to turn back over.

"Shit." Azem hisses.

I sit up with him.

"She never calls me." He swipes his finger across the bottom of his mother's picture. "Is everything ok?" Azem pulls his hair back from his forehead and releases a breath. "Your mom's here."

VII

Snot threatens to spill out of my right nostril while I bend over my duffel bag looking for clothes. I yank my jeans on and pull a hoodie on.

Azem stands an arm's length away from me with his hands on his hips.

I hop into one of my Nikes when I hear Azem talking.

"Calm down, baby. You have to be calm when you go up there."

I know he's right, but it doesn't help simmer my boiling blood.

"Why the hell is she here?" I ask the air. After I thumb my foot into my untied shoe, Azem pulls me over to him by the waistband of my blond denim skinny jeans.

"Zoe, don't go off," Azem keeps me in place until I stop and listen to him.

"I hear you Azem." I look into his beautiful face to memorize every inch of his perfect, smooth face. His long dimple peeks out as he searches my face for sanity.

"Please, be calm." He advises.

I throw my body into his. My feet never touch the ground while he squeezes me. He places me back down long before I want to stop.

When I make it to the front door, Zara and Roger are watching my mom on the other side of the screen door. I try not to linger on the sorrow I notice in their eyes. They walk away into a nearby room.

"What the hell did I tell you?" Mom says. She must have run out of the benevolence she's known for at work. There's never anything good left for me. It shouldn't surprise me anymore.

"Mom, come inside, so we don't have to talk through the door." I push the gold-framed screen door wide for her. Fog blooms on the surface of the gold gilded screen door. It's too cold to have a standoff with her right here, but her stubbornness will not allow her to back down.

"You need to get your stuff so we can go."

I can feel Azem's strong body before he reaches us at the door.

"Please Ms. Mason. We would love it if you stepped in to talk. There's food and."

She cuts him off. "I am not here to talk. I am here to pick my daughter up."

He looks down at the floor before he steps back.

"Mom, I'll be home soon. You don't need to make a scene."

"Zoe, go inside, get your shit, and let's go." Hearing her disrespect Azem's family in the threshold of their own home, makes me snap.

Azem catches me before I have a chance to lay into her.

He steps between us and walks me back a few steps. He pulls my face up to his. "Zoe, I love you. Don't do it." He warns.

I can't help crying. I don't want to leave him.

"You are my very life. Please, don't fight with your mom. It's ok, I've already got my gift for Christmas." He takes my left hand in his and thumbs my ring finger.

He isn't convincing me to leave, but I can't argue with him. I love him too much.

Instead of kissing me, he goes downstairs to get my bag. When he gets back, he stands between us again.

"Go, Zoe."

He moves to my side, and I take my duffel bag from his fingers. He drapes my coat over my shoulders.

I refuse to look at her on the ride home. She conspires with somebody on her phone.

"Yes. She's here. Thank you for staying up for me. I'll call you in the morning. Ok. Bye."

I hate how she's fooling that idiot on the phone with her into thinking she's a nice person.

"And get used to the chauffeur because your car is gone." She adds.

"How am I supposed to get to work?" I make no effort to hide the disgust in my voice. She's too full of her own shit to notice that I'm not fucking around either.

"I can arrange something for you. Give me your schedule and I'll have a ride lined up for you."

I'll walk home before I step foot into anything she's got lined up for me.

"You're doing all this because I spent Christmas with Azem?"

She looks at me like I'm one of her burned victims.

"I warned you Zoe, and you did it anyway." She shakes her head at me, then focuses on the road again.

She doesn't talk for the rest of the ride home, and I wish it could stay that way.

I throw my bag down in the kitchen. I'm not wasting my time getting comfortable. She's in attack mode, and I need to be ready.

She follows me to the kitchen. She clanks a wine glass against the counter and fills it to the brim.

I wish I would've left the water in that wine bottle now. It would've been fun to see her lose it when she goes to take a long drag of piss warm tap water.

She stares me down WWE style while she attempts to fill her goblet. Half of the white wine splashes on the countertop. She doesn't seem to care, as long as she has something to make her little show more dramatic.

She downs the wine like an athlete on a Gatorade commercial. Wine dribbles down the sides of her mouth. She backhands the wet streams off her face, then pours another glass.

It's exhausting standing here watching her become the lush my dad was. If she wants to stare me down, it's going to be with my ass resting on the kitchen table.

Azem has my muscles fatigued for the best reason. He may have been a virgin coming into this relationship, but he's been an expert from day one. He makes me happier than I've ever been in my life. My mom has to see it on me.

"Since you've chosen to live life according to Zoe, it's time for me to show you how my program works."

She pours another glass, spilling most of it on the counter.

"As I've already informed you, your car is as good as sold as far as you're concerned.

"I heard you in the car." I snap.

"Don't try it, Zoe, cause I'm not in the mood for this shit tonight."

That makes two of us.

She jabs her finger at me.

"Since you, refuse to stay away from that damned boy, you need to see what they do to girls like you where he's from.

She stumbles away. When comes back, she has her ragtag laptop. I'm surprised she can access the Internet at all on that thing. She's always complaining about the Internet, but her outdated computer is the problem. Her laptop is the Atari of laptops, and not in a good way. The charger cord trundles behind her as she crosses the kitchen for the table. She fumbles with the cord for a long time before she finds the prongs in the outlet on the wall.

"Sit down."

Her eyes are bloodshot as her voice strains. When I don't move, she jumps to her feet and sticks her Riesling laced breath in my face.

I hold my breath. Her breath smells like recycled vomit.

"Sit down." I can hear Azem's promises to me in my mind. If only he could be here where the real threat to my safety is.

Mom works like a maniac on her laptop.

Before I can register what she's pulled up, her fingers strangle my neck. She forces my head close to the screen.

"Look at what Azem's kind, do to women."

Her voice is going hoarse with all her tough talk. Her iron grip doesn't let up a bit as I raise my eyes to the screen.

My vision is blurry. It's impossible to read the English subtitles until my tears fall out the way. I try to pry my head away from the screen, but she's too strong. I would put up more of a fight if her knife-sharp nails weren't digging into the sides of my neck.

Fury suffocates me.

"You can't make me watch this." I close my eyes, but not for long. The second my eyelids close, her nails dig in more. I try to pry her stick-thin fingers away, but her grip only gets tighter.

"Stop scratching me," I yelp. I wish Azem was here to help me. Unbeknownst to him, he was feeding me right into the tiger's mouth. Despite the pain that I'm in, I don't blame Azem for this. The responsibility for this lunacy rests on my mom's shoulders.

She hammers the volume key until it's on max.

"The sooner you sit still the sooner you can get this over with."

I loosen my grip on her fingers and look at the screen. The images before me will never leave my mind. It should be my choice to watch this, not her punishment. She's no better than any of the men hurling stones at the bagged woman.

"You need to see this." My mom grunts. "Do you know what her offense was?" She quizzes me.

A tear slips down my face.

"The same thing you were doing with that boy tonight." She answers for me.

When the woman is dead, I struggle to get up.

"No, her boyfriend is next. Spittle flies out the side of her mouth onto my cheek. I'm sick to my stomach. I don't know why she's doing this to me.

When my mom's satisfied that the bloody bag that the man is in has enough stones heaped on top, she releases me.

I can't believe that her nails didn't break my skin. I keep pulling my fingers away from my neck to check them for blood, but there's nothing but half moon indents.

She lunges up from her seat at the kitchen table.

"Go get your phone, and drop it inside."

I stand up and walk to my bag, still grasping my neck with one hand. The home screen is full of texts from Azem. I can't hold my tears back when I see his name. I need him so bad right now.

I drop the phone inside, and she zips the bag up like a detective on Law and Order. "If you need to use the phone, you may use my phone. "This," she says wiggling the bag in front of her stupid face, "is going back to the store."

There's a sickening smile on her face as she pinches the bag closed. Rage erupts inside of me, but there's no point in doing anything about it. She's a full out lunatic and I don't want to see any other moves she has.

"You do not leave this house unless it's on fire. I have ways of knowing everything so if you want to test me, try it. "Good night."

She takes the last glass of wine to the head straight from the bottle, then takes her laptop and my phone to her room.

The first thing I do is look at my pathetic face in the mirror. My neck throbs, my eyes are bloodshot, my nose is running, and I'm wearing humiliation like the sack that woman died in.

The sunny side of Christmas morning feels like a funeral. I dread the idea of getting out of bed and facing life with my mom again. I wish she had a million patients to see today. She's never off on Christmas. My stomach turns to liquid when she bursts into my room.

"Merry Christmas Zoe. Come get something to eat."

She bounces out of my room like the psycho she is.

She's like a completely different person. If my neck wasn't still sore, there wouldn't be any evidence that she went mental on me last night.

I pray that she doesn't have a stoning video for us to wash our pancakes down with this morning.

"Two or three pancakes?" She's Polly Homemaker this morning.

I agree to eat one.

She shakes her head, still smiling. "That's my Zo." She says, sliding one chocolate chip pancake onto my plate.

I sit down and eye her laptop. I pretend to sip my orange juice until it's safe to eat the pancake that hits my stomach like stones.

After we eat, we open presents.

She gifts me a bounty of Chanel makeup. I don't want anything from her. I got her a gold stethoscope. She tears up when she opens it. I have to check my body against a flinch when she hugs and kisses me. I try a toothless smile before she turns around to trash the wrapping paper. I wipe her kiss off my face before she turns back around.

When Christmas time is over, I race back to my room and bury myself underneath the covers. I miss Azem with a bitterness that threatens to make breakfast come back up.

"Zoe, I have work tonight. I've already taken more time than I can afford to take. There are people watching you, so do not think that you can leave this house. If I find out you did, you will be un-enrolled from that school, and you'll finish the year out online."

Every word her filthy mouth says makes me sicker. She is completely nuts. Polly Homemaker smiles at me again, then closes my door.

With every passing minute, I'm more desperate. I need to see Azem, without getting caught. I suspect my perverted neighbor across the street ratted us out. Even Mr. Nosey across the backyard wouldn't go as far as tailing someone. Only the nasty bastard across the street would do something that desperate.

All he needed as payment was a couple of smiles and a full view of my mom's ass.

I know there are rules about honoring your father and mother, but don't they have to be honorable in the first place? I can't let go of what she did. She did not have to show me that gruesome video. I'm not a fool, I've heard of the atrocities that come out of that region of the world.

I noticed that my next-door neighbor's car in the driveway. We hung out on the odd Friday when she went to Easton. We settled for each other when we couldn't find anyone better to hang out with. I hate to admit it, but I need her help. She's the real expert here after all. Before my mom turned into a complete psycho, I was always free to hang out. I never had to rebel, since mom's schedule gave me all the freedom in the world to party.

Jordan was always in trouble for something. Even though she was a year older than me, she always worshipped how much freedom I had. I felt more like an orphan at the time, but I wasn't going to tell her as much.

I dress in black from head to toe, like a burglar. I creep through my backyard over to hers. I pray that the perv across the street is too busy being disgusting to notice me in the backyard. I palm the concrete patio slab around the perimeters of her house for rocks. The cold and jagged edges scratch my knuckles. I break two nails before I can find three pebbles small enough to throw. No matter what I do, everything reminds me of that video. I'll never think of rocks the same way again.

The first rock pings off her the edge of her window. I hunker down to keep as much of my shadow off of the moonlit patio slab as possible.

No answer.

The second rock goes up.

Still nothing.

I fling the last rock at the window.

I'm peering over the side of her house to run back to my side when I hear a window scrolling up. She looks down and makes eye contact with me. Without saying a word, she closes the window.

Seconds later the patio door slides open for me to slip inside.

I ask her to use her phone.

She doesn't ask any questions. She takes me upstairs to her room, hands over her Samsung, and closes the door tight behind her.

It's amazing how valuable her experience as a prisoner has come full circle. I don't trust anyone to help me sneak around more than I trust her right now.

Azem answers on the first ring.

"Zoe?" Azem's voice sounds ragged.

I try to say something back, but I can't for the whimpers that suspend my voice.

"Zoe? What's wrong? Tell me what's going on." Azem's measured words struggle under his anxiety. "I'm going over there," Azem yells in the background.

Zara's on the phone next. "Zoe, love, are you alright?" Her words make me cry more.

"Shhh, Zoe. Shhh, Azem, it's ok, give her a few moments. Calm down Azem." She coaches the two of us.

My throat finally clears enough for me to speak.

"I'm sorry," I say.

"No apologies, we want to know..." Her voice fades to the background, then Azem's back on the phone.

"I'm fine," I say.

"You're not fine." Azem's patience is gone. "What happened to you last night? And don't tell me nothing."

"My mom was mad that's all."

Azem doesn't press me any further. He exhales.

"What's this number you're calling me from?"

"It's my next door neighbor's."

"Your mom took your phone?"

"Yes."

"For how long?"

"I can't have it back."

"I'm coming over there," Azem insists.

"No. You can't."

"Zoe, we can talk to her together," pleads Azem.

"She's not going to listen. She took my car too."

Every spoonful of crazy I give Azem drives him more insane.

"She forbade you?" He sounds so wounded.

"It can't last forever. I'll be eighteen in a few months, then I can leave this hell hole." I say.

"So I can't see you until school's back in?"

Somehow I'm falling deeper in love with Azem at the same time my heart shatters. My silence answers him.

"Can I call this phone for you?"

"She's cool, but no, I'll call you."

"How can I know you're safe?"

"I'm fine. I'll be fine." My voice wavers.

"Zoe, this is crazy." He says.

I can't speak again because he's right.

"How can I bring in the New Year without my bride?" He hisses.

I have to end this call.

I can only imagine the kind of gossip I'm feeding Jordan right now.

"I'll call you by then. I have to go."

"I love you, Zoe."

"I love you too." I push the red button and spend an eon wiping tears off my face. Before I can finish, Jordan comes back in the room.

Still mouse silent, she leads me out of her room and down creaky steps to the patio door. At the patio door, she finally speaks.

"If you come over on New Year's Eve, I'll take you where ever you want to go."

I can't look at her. She has no shame left, after the way her parents shackled her. I wouldn't blame her if she has a good laugh about all this when I leave. Once upon a time, her situation seemed pretty comical to me too.

She surprises me when she bends down and hugs me. She wastes no time opening the patio door so I can sneak back out.

My heartbeat doesn't slow down until I'm undressed and back under my covers in bed.

VIII

The week of New Year's Eve, my mom obsesses over work too much to torture me. Even still I have zero motivation. I don't have any schoolwork to distract me. Most of my time revolves around devising ways to use the phone every day.

My mom drives me to work the two days that I'm scheduled. She chose right by taking me to work because I was going to skip work both days to see Azem.

Driving home with my mom as she babbles on about work is miserable. The only thing that would make me feel better is seeing Azem.

I never confirmed with Jordan that I would take her up on her offer to sneak me out. It doesn't matter because she's ready when I show up on her patio.

When I step inside, she's holding a wig. My top lip curls at the black monstrosity dangling from her long fingers.

"I'm not wearing that." I protest.

She shrugs and stuffs it into her drawstring purse.

"It'll be here if you change your mind."

I almost laugh with her. It's the first smiling I've done in several days.

I ride to Azem's house with my head in my lap.

Jordan doesn't bat an eyelash while she drives. She's the best get away driver I've ever seen. Her focus is unwavering. She leaves her Samsung with me, so she can text me when she's on her way to pick me back up.

Jordan doesn't waste any time peeling off as soon as I'm out the car.

Azem's stands in the driveway waiting for me. It takes everything I have not to barrel him over when we hug.

Zara and Roger take turns hugging me inside. I struggle to keep it all together the tighter their hugs get. As soon as Roger lets me go, Azem takes me straight downstairs. A week ago, he never would have tried a move like this. He's obviously convinced Zara and Roger how much he loves me.

Azem and I undress each other. He picks me up and carries me to his bed. He pulls the comforter back and slides me underneath. He slips in next, and our arms lock around each other.

Sobs make my body shake in his arms.

"You're nobody's prisoner. It isn't right what your mother's doing." He kisses my forehead down to my nose then lips.

"It doesn't matter, I'll be eighteen soon." My rasp.

Azem wipes my face. "Zoe, it doesn't matter, wrong is wrong. "What does she have against me?"

My heart shatters again.

I've only got a few hours of freedom. I don't want to spend it talking about my mom's psychosis. I take a breath in through my nose and exhale it through my nose. I refuse to think about that damned stoning video again.

"My mom is a control freak. Always has been. She's throwing her weight around because it's slipping away from her. She says she'll pull me out of Easton, and refuses to help me with college if I disobey her. She's freaking, because I'm out of here when school is over, and she knows it. The only thing that gets me through all the drama, is you."

Azem drops the subject. I know that he's far from finished.

"Did you miss me?" I say. I'm gasping for breath while Azem smothers me with his broad chest. I love every inch of his weight pressing in on me.

"Stop." Azem licks inside the well of my ear.

"Show me how much you missed me." I moan.

Azem speeds up. "Zoe, I don't want to finish right now, you feel so good." Azem slows down again.

I missed you, so much."

His body disobeys him and spasms with hard jerks.

We hug for longer than we have sex. Even more than the sex, I miss his touch. I don't know how I'm going to go without it again.

I straddle him while he sits up. When I cry again, he rocks me in his lap until I calm down.

Azem leaves a hickey in my left inner thigh so I'll have something to remember him by.

"Give me one." He says pointing to his neck.

"I can't leave a hickey on your neck," I say.

"My neck belongs to you. Do it. I want some ink anyway. Your love bite will tell me if I like having art so high up."

"I didn't know you were into tattoos," I flinch at the thought. I've always had a secret fetish for heavy tattooing. "What about your mom, and getting a job?" I say laughing out loud.

"What's so funny? He says crooking his head around to look in my eyes.

I shake my head. "Nothing. I shouldn't tell you this, but ink is sexy as hell."

"It's settled. I'm definitely getting inked up." He declares.

"What's inspired you so much to get tatted?"

"You." He says.

"What do you mean me?"

"I mean, it's one of the best ways I can think of to show you how much I love you."

He is dead serious.

"So every tattoo you get will be to me?" I say.

"Every one." He pulls my head in toward his neck, but I can't believe this.

"How much work do you want?"

"My neck on both sides at least, my chest, sides of my lower stomach, and both sleeves. I'm not against my legs, but I want to start my upper body first."

I smile and try to coax the joke out of him. "You're not serious."

"Dead serious." He says. "Don't worry, I'll make plenty of money. Now, will you please start my bite? Make it good." He closes his eyes and cocks his head to the side.

I bring in the New Year straddling Azem's lap and sucking the best love bite I can into his neck.

His bite stands out bright and red on his neck.

Azem admires his first tattoo while I dry off.

I laugh at his enthusiasm as he stands back and flexes his tight body in the mirror.

"How are you going to get a job with ink all over your body?" I ask.

He turns around and leans one leg on his dresser. "I'm opening up a Calisthenics gym after high school." He says.

"You don't want to go to college?" I say wiping beads of water off the back of my neck.

Azem shrugs. "I don't see the point in wasting the time or money."

I knew Azem wanted to do something interesting after high school, but I would never have guessed it was this.

"Why Calisthenics?" I say.

"We didn't have much back East, so I used my own body weight to add resistance to the workouts I did. That's all Calisthenics is. After about two years, I had a system that was making me ripped, without lifting any weight. There never was too much food to go around, so creating a caloric deficit was easy. It's much more tempting to stay on track now, but I'm getting used to it."

I've always admired how disciplined he seems, now I know that it wasn't my imagination. I am beyond impressed. I don't know if it's the distance my mom is forcing on us or not, but Azem's like an open book tonight and I can't get enough of it. His confidence is so impressive.

He smiles. "What are you thinking?" He says.

"I love to hear you talking about your plans for the future," I reply.

"I won't consider any of it if I don't have you." He says penetrating me with that dark stare of his.

"Why?"

I know he's irritated with my insecurity, but I can't help it. I imagine him with his tight tattooed body, and symmetrical face, and I don't get it. I'm five foot three, with a minute's worth of hair. I can't be more normal. He meets me and takes my hand. We walk to his full body mirror next to the bathroom door. He tips the black oval mirror down until I can see my whole body. He holds me by the nodes on the sides of my pelvis.

"Zoe, you're perfect to me. Your face is beautiful without anything on it. Before this year I wouldn't have believed a woman could be so pretty with hair like yours. I get upset when I see other women with short hair because I know that my baby does it the best. I wish I could figure out a way to patent your hairstyle so no other woman can copy you. Haven't you noticed how many girls at school have ripped your hairstyle off?"

I turn around to look at his real face, but he turns me back to my reflection.

"I've never seen any other girls with their hair like this at school."

"Well, there are a lot of them now. When you notice them, don't tell me just tally it up. There's at least ten in our class alone. Anyway, your body is tight, slender, and perfection in all the spots that count. I love how you fit in my hands. He cups my breasts, then turns me around and fits both hands over my butt. You're too sexy to see it yourself, but trust me everybody else can. I've been two seconds off kicking some ass at school over guys looking at you, or trying to push up on you."

I can't believe the words that are coming out of Azem's mouth. Not only is he gorgeous, but he wants to marry me. Screw dating or even having a perpetual engagement. He wants his ring on my finger. If we could, I would go to Vegas tonight.

I can't stand leaving him tonight, but this will not have to be our reality forever.

The only thing that helps me out of Azem's house, is everything he told me tonight. Knowing that Azem refuses to start his future without me in it is the best thing that he could've said to me.

I creep back over to my house and slide back inside the patio door. I take two steps in the kitchen before my mom clears her throat. She's sitting in the dark waiting for me at the table. I keep moving, hoping that I can make it to my room before she can catch up. She leaps up out of her chair and follows me, but she doesn't rush. She stalks behind me like Jason. She's scaring the shit out of me moseying through the house like this.

I pull my black leather bomber jacket off. She got it for me for Christmas. The only reason it's touching my skin is that it's sneak out of the house black. I keep my combat boots on.

"Where were you?" Mom's so angry that there isn't any anger in her voice.

"I was with Jordan," I say.

She stares at me for an eternity before she charges at me like a wild bull. She attempts to push me against the wall, but I dodge to the right. I catch a pinky finger in corner of my left eye. There's no time for me to cradle my burning, injured eye because she's after me again. This time she catches me from behind and slams my head down on the vanity. It feels like she's trying to flatten my face like the pancakes she made on Christmas morning.

"I told you not to leave the damn house! I don't give a damn if it was next door."

I flail my legs, trying to gain enough leverage to lift her off my body. I make a mental note to have Azem teach me Calisthenics. I bet he has enough strength to get out of this hold. Hell, he wouldn't be in this position in the first place. I almost zone completely out, thinking about him.

She gives my head one more excruciating smash for good luck, then steps back. The nut job that used to be my mom centers the gold stethoscope around her neck. She tucks the loose strands from her bun back up.

"Go to bed." She pants then leaves.

I've never been happier to go back to school in my life. The ride to school with my mom is only bearable because I'll be away from her soon. She warns me to come straight home after school. I nod at her, and all but run away from the car.

Zero hour saves me from Azem seeing me. I spend the entire time in zero hour devising a strategy to hide the strawberry red blood clot in my eye. It's only in the corner, but if he sees it, he'll flip.

I thank God that he's already in his seat when I arrive at first hour. It's a miracle that my seat is in front of his. It's the perfect cover to hide my eye. I turn to my right and sneak a look at him. He gives me a tight smile back. His hickey is darker and stands out on his neck. He wears it like a badge of honor. He doesn't know how taboo hickeys are in the States. Even if he did, he wouldn't care. Everybody's had one, but after the ninth grade, most people avoid them like the plague. I haven't had one since eighth grade. Covering my hickey was my first real introduction to makeup.

Azem and I keep a low profile at school. He says he only does it for me. He wants everybody to know that he belongs to me, but I'm afraid of what Hendrat will do.

Other than the real threat of Hendrat, it's next to impossible to kiss Azem in front of an audience. Azem isn't the guy you can give a mindless peck to.

I pretend to rub my left eye while we talk after class. He's used to me keeping it short and sweet in the hallway. I walk away as more people start paying attention to us.

At lunch, I sit to his left and rest my fist against my face. I'm trying my best to look normal. When Azem's tired of watching me pick over the food on my tray. He stacks our trays and stands up to take them to the trashcan.

He scares me half to death when he zooms into the chair on my other side. He pulls my hand from my face and examines my eye.

"Who did this to you?" Azem's using his don't bullshit me voice which turns me on more than it should.

My left eye stings like a bitch as tears well up in my eyes.

"Your mom?" His voice is one octave above a growl. "Zoe?" Azem's face scrunches up a hundred different ways as he struggles to figure out why I'm so stupid. His face softens. "Do you have all your stuff?"

I nod.

"Let's go." He takes my hand in his and secures his fingers between mine. He leads me through a sea of students in the cafeteria. If I cared about anything other than him, I would notice that people are already gossiping about us. This is the first rumor about us that they'll get right. Even if Azem weren't on a mission, he would proudly walk down the hall hand in hand with me. It isn't until now, that I realize how stupid I've been to hide my love for him. We've likely loved each other since the first minute we met.

Azem breaks most of Easton's rules leaving school with me, but he doesn't care. His alpha swag definitely makes more sense now that I know his plans to ink up and start a Calisthenics gym.

Somehow the prism of these two aspects of his personality makes things clearer. Azem takes absolutely no shit and doesn't enslave himself to the rules of the herd. In class, he does the work, but he doesn't care about the grades. His perfectionist way about him always gets him the A, but the alpha in him could care less about it.

Azem doesn't let me go for a second until we're in the car. When he's inside, he takes my hand back before he speeds off.

IX

"I would say fuck everything in there, but if you're anything like my mom, I know you can't do that." Azem shifts his car into park. He still has my hand in his lap. I can feel him through his gray joggers. It's hard to pay attention with my hand against him like this. "Get what you need so we can get out of here." Azem grinds his teeth together when he looks at my eye again. He flicks his head toward his door. "Come on."

He meets me at my side and closes my car door tight behind me.

I almost tell Azem about the perv across the street, but I don't trust that Azem won't cripple him.

Azem's lean body stands inside the threshold of my door with one arm leaning against the frame. He keeps reaching inside the pocket of his gray joggers to look at his phone.

"I've got an appointment in an hour. Get what you need for now, and we'll come back later to get everything else." He pockets his iPhone again. When he does, the side of his joggers dips down, and the v on his pelvis shows.

"Where's your appointment?" I say.

He shakes his head, and his hair unravels from atop his head. "For one, I need a cut, then I've got to take care of some other things." Azem's coal black eyes are unblinking.

"Is it a secret?" I say, bending over my bed for my stray New Balance tennis shoe. He stares at my butt and bites down on his lower lip.

"No secret, but I don't want to tell you. Not yet." Azem shifts his pants right where the cords dangle in front of his crotch.

I stand back up and scan the room.

"Ready?" Azem glances down the hallway.

I join him at the door. "I can't stay the night with you Azem, my mom's going to pull me out of Easton."

Azem takes the Nike duffel bag from my hand.

"Yes you can, and no she won't," Azem says then follows me out my room.

"Let's get married on May 1st." Azem's voice slices through the silence in the car.

"Why?"

Azem stops the car in the middle of the street. He turns on me. "Zoe, I thought we already had this conversation."

The blaring horns drive me crazy.

"Will you pull over?"

Azem glances out his side view mirror and waves the cars off. "I don't care about them. I want to know why you don't think I mean what I say?" Azem is dead serious.

I try to block out the deafening sounds of people laying on their horns. "I only asked why, because."

"You think I pity you." Azem cuts me off.

I look down at my hands.

"Isn't it?" Azem demands.

I suck my breath in when I start to cry. My left eye hurts so bad.

Azem finally pulls the car over to the side of the road.

"I want to marry you on May first because I told you I want to marry you when we can make independent decisions. I was going to say let's do it after graduation, but I don't see the point waiting another month. You are my first, last, and only, I am your first last and only. My birthday is February first, yours is April first. May first is the right day. That's all. It's not pity for what your mom did to you. Which by the way, if she was a man, I would be fucking her up right now."

I pull my hands away from my face and glance at Azem. He's staring out his driver's side window.

"I love it. I love you." I say.

Azem lunges to my side of the car and pulls me against him as tight as I can take it.

"I'll be right back." Azem places the remote control in my lap. He kisses my forehead. It finally dawns on me that he kisses me on the forehead to prevent from tearing my clothes off. Any other time we're alone, we don't stop.

My body caves in on itself as soon as he leaves. I thought that I was getting too much sleep at home but in reality, I had to sleep with one eye open. I only see a few minutes of the episode of Walking Dead before I fall asleep.

When I wake up to Azem massaging my feet. He winks at me and I shiver. I've done nothing to deserve a guy this fine. His haircut is perfect. The sides and back are tapered down low. The top is still long, but a few centimeters shorter. I love that his hair still falls over his forehead in n irresistible tangle. He replaced his long-sleeved gray t-shirt for a black Under Armour hoodie. His black tapered joggers accent his muscled lower body like they were tailor-made.

"Here." Azem hands me a black iPhone box. I spring up on the couch. I stare at him and the phone bug-eyed.

"I don't know what I was thinking, but I should have got you another one a long time ago. You're on our plan now." He says looking up over his head at the ceiling. "I'd like to see your mom try to take that." Says Azem.

Years ago, I would hate hearing someone talk about my mom. Azem is a different story. At barely eighteen he's all man. He's zero percent bullshit. He brims over with testosterone, and heart. I knew he wasn't joking when he said he would kick my mom's ass if she were a man.

"My mom wants you to have this." He dangles a key ring with a large gold number one and a single key attached. I ignore my stinging eye when a tear falls free.

"She wants to give you some space. She said there's plenty of time to talk when you get back home."

I crawl into Azem's lap. I wrap my arms around his neck.

"Thank you."

His neck smells like alcohol.

Azem flinches away from me.

I notice some kind of plastic stuck to his neck.

Azem peels a corner of the tape and plastic away.

"I found one of your blot things in the bathroom after school one day, and kept it for this."

On his neck is a tattoo of my lips in the same cinnamon color I always wear. It's in the same spot where I sucked a hickey on his neck. The hickey was still on his neck when he got the tattoo.

"Do you like it?" Azem asks nervously.

"I love it," I say.

"Good, then you'll love this one too." Azem pushes the wrapping back down on his neck, then squirms out of his hoodie. Above his left peck, there's a tattoo of my name. He even had the tattoo artist include the umlaut. The only teacher at my school who honored the correct spelling of my name was Mr. Webb. I'm tempted to touch the swollen dark lettering on his chest but I know better. My name is so sexy on his chest. The Z has long flowing lines and sharp peaks. The capital Z is three times as big as the other two letters. The o and e nestle inside the cove of the greater than sign the Z makes. I help him press his protective covering back on his ink and get his hoodie back on.

Azem and I eat dinner downstairs. He assures me that his mom doesn't mind that we're not eating with them

"This is literally my part of the house Zoe. You can walk around naked down here, and she'd never know." He winks.

I drop my fork, stand up, and strip out of my clothes. I walk around the basement, careful to take my time. I can feel Azem's eyes following me. I try to do a full lap around the basement, but Azem catches me around the waist before I can pass him. He nibbles my stomach between his teeth, then looks up from the couch.

"What do you think you're doing?" Azem says.

"I'm walking around the basement naked, silly." I try to get out of his grip, but he holds on tighter, still gnawing on my stomach.

"I want you to eat some more." He says.

"Ok." I push his head back and take my seat next to him again. I pick up a forkful of Salmon and pop it in my mouth.

Azem leans back on the couch. "Zoe, I can't eat with you like that."

I look at him over my shoulder, and his eyes shimmer.

When we re-emerge from the bedroom, our food is as cold as ice. Azem heats everything back up and commands me to keep my clothes on this time.

"All I meant by that, is she respects my privacy, even more since you're here." Azem scrapes the last of the quinoa into his mouth.

"Ok," I reply.

Azem shakes his head at me. He rakes his hair back.

"I love your hair like that," I say.

"I was beginning to worry you didn't like it." Azem downs a whole bottle of water in one pass.

"I'm sorry that you'll have to take me to school so early," I say.

Azem snaps his fingers then leaps up off the couch. He brings back another key with a BMW logo on it, and a black garage door opener.

"I'm not driving that," I say.

"I'm not the one you have to tell."

Azem shakes his semi-wavy hair loose, then sweeps it back again. I love how he plays in his hair. He tosses the key and garage door opener on the coffee table and leans back again.

"I planned on us driving to school together. This car is for everything else you want to do."

I can't believe his mom's generosity. I can't believe much of anything.

Both Azem and I sensed that my mom would pull her next stunt at Easton. As soon as Azem and I walk in the entrance door I see my mom through the glass windows in the office. My mom looks as peaceful as the First Lady of a church. I can feel Azem's tension when he reaches around me to open the office door.

My mom looks at Azem like he's a joke. The closer we get to her, the smugger the look on her face gets.

"Say your goodbyes." She says in our general direction.

Her eyes return to Hendrat's closed office door.

"Should we go to the car to get the copy of the police report we filed yesterday for your little meeting?"

Azem jabs his thumb behind him. His torso flexes rock solid behind me. His question dissolves her tough front.

"Zoe?" My mom looks at me wounded.

I concentrate on Azem instead.

"The sergeant told us to carry it at all times in the event we need proof of the incident. Let Hendrix know that we have a copy of the abuse kit too if he wants to have a look at it."

For once my mom has nothing to say, but the stark fear in her eyes says it all.

She stands up. "I have a right to know what's going on with my daughter." She whines.

Hendrat, rigid and cold as ever strides toward us. He looks irritated that Ms. Horn isn't around to take care of us for him.

"Good morning Mrs. Mason, right this way." He holds out a stiff arm toward his office.

"I apologize, I'm on call at work. I'm an RN at Regional. The hospital needs me to come in right away. I'll call to reschedule." She scuttles past us. Her vanilla bean body lotion trails behind her.

"Alright then. Have a good day, students." He eyes the two of us suspiciously before he stalks back to his office.

Azem nods toward the lobby door and we jog out to the parking lot.

"We'll be there this evening to get the rest of Zoe's stuff," Azem says twenty paces away from my mom.

My mom turns around like an Android. I can tell that she's close to losing her shit right here on the school parking lot.

"Or we could follow the sergeant's advice and bring a police escort with us." If Azem was playing poker he would be winning an all-in bet with the best bluff in the world.

"Zoe knows she's always welcome home." My mom says retreating inside her car.

"Good we'll see you this evening." Azem faces me. "Come on baby."

When we get back inside, Azem and I race down to the basement. He hugs me until my anxiety goes away. "I love you, Zoe. I'm sorry about all that, but I had a feeling your mom was going to try that shit. I will never lie to you." He kisses me until the first bell for zero hour rings.

X

"Don't take anything you didn't pay for." My mom shouts as soon as Azem and I step through the front door. She stands at the top of the steps with a mug of wine. There's no use hiding it now, especially after the way she's been torturing me.

I wish I didn't have to pretend to be strong right now. Azem is right. I should leave everything here.

Azem stands inside my bedroom door while I pack my clothes and shoes.

"Nope, I bought that." She yells.

I look at the purse in my hand and release its handle. It falls to the floor. At this rate, I'm never going to finish packing. I remember most of the clothes I purchased, but apparently, any gifts she bought me were on loan. I try not to notice how the tips of Azem's ears are turning red.

"I bought those jeans last year. You said you would pay me back and never did." My mom spouts.

Azem moves away from the door. "Zoe, we're leaving."

"I'm not leaving my stuff here." I know I sound like an infant, but I don't care.

"Yeah, cause you can't come back." My mom says.

Azem turns around on her. I pull on his t-shirt. He shakes his head at her then focuses on me again. "Zoe, don't take this from her. I can replace everything in here."

"That's not the point," I say.

Azem sweeps his hair back and rests his hand on the top of his head.

I resume packing. I don't touch anything that I can't remember buying.

When she disappears from the doorway, I stuff all of "her" items in my bag anyway.

Azem doesn't leave me alone for a second.

We pack Roger's Range Rover. When Azem has my last two overstuffed bags in one hand my mom blocks the doorway to my room.

"So you sell your mom out for some dick?"

I step in front of Azem. He's trying to hold me back.

"Goodbye Claire," I say.

My mom's face blanches at the sound of her name coming out of my mouth.

I'll have to ask Azem if it's as blasphemous in his culture to call his mother by her first name the way it is here in the U. S.

She's so off-kilter that she moves out of the way so we can pass by.

"Nobody will love you like your mother does. I promise you that. You'll be back as soon as he hurts your little feelings."

The more she speaks the more pathetic she sounds.

"Are you alright?" Azem asks as he cranks the truck up.

"No."

I can't stop staring at my mom standing behind the screen door as we drive away.

My sorrow disappears when I remember what she's become.

"You had to get out of there Zoe. It was only going to get worse."

Coming from anyone else, I may not listen, but Azem knows what he's talking about. His family life was so tragic that he and his mom had to flee to another continent.

Azem, Zara, and Roger are no longer the family I wish I could be a part of. They're all I have now. As hard as it is to face my own problems right now, I know I have to ask what Azem and his mom escaped from. Even Roger seems wounded by what's happened to Zara and Azem.

Zara doesn't ask us how it went when we get back. She can tell that I'm not in good shape.

Azem and I have dinner at the kitchen table with Zara and Roger instead of at the center island. After Zara clears the dishes away, she returns to the table. The moment the question leaves my mouth, I know that nothing between the four of us will ever be the same.

Zara, Azem, and Roger take turns looking at each other. Both Zara and Azem feel thousands of miles away. Still, Azem pulls me closer to him. Roger sits back while Zara remains erect on the edge of her seat.

When Zara begins her story, I understand why Roger looks like he'd would rather be anywhere but here.

Azem doesn't share much more than he already has with me. I can tell he wants to forget that any of the horrific things Zara's explaining ever happened to them.

There's so much information to absorb, that I have too many questions for Zara to answer in one sitting. I also get the sense that Zara is only giving me a glimpse of their former life. I'm grateful that she stops when she does. Sitting through an hour of their life back East has me nauseous.

"Please follow me," Zara says after she puts a pin in the horror movie that used to be her and Azem's life. Azem looks uneasy when she opens the door to the basement and walks downstairs. I look back at him, and he hunches his shoulders. Please don't let her have a talk with us about all the sex we've been having.

She opens the door to a room across the hall from Azem's. When she opens the door, the first thing that comes to mind is cinnamon.

Roger, Azem and I stand at the door like the Three Stooges. Azem's definitely Shemp, the way he's constantly sweeping his hair out of his face. I giggle at the thought. Azem and Roger look down at me like I've lost my mind.

This room is beautiful. It's as grand as Azem's across the hall. It's the exact color of the cinnamon lip gloss I wear most days. I didn't realize it was my favorite color until now. The vanity is in the same cinnamon color. The comforter, drapes, carpet, and lampshades are all cinnamon. Zara smiles at me. Her pride makes her eyes gleam.

I smile back at her.

She walks over to me and takes my hand in hers. She stands in front of the vanity table.

"Sit." She instructs.

I sit down.

It isn't until I look at my reflection in the mirror that everything clicks.

"Zara." I hug Azem's mom tight.

She hugs me back tighter.

"For you love. I want you to have any and everything you need to have a good life. I'm so sorry you're going through this. You'll have everything you need here. The only thing that will upset me is if you don't ask me for help anytime you need it. It doesn't matter what it is, I'll see to it that you have it." Zara jets out the room before I can say anything. I now know to let her go.

"Welcome, Zoe. I'm glad you're here." Roger says. His hug smothers me in the best way. He flicks Azem's hair back out of place. Azem tries to dodge him, but Roger's long arms reach him anyway.

Azem doesn't look amused. He stands at the door with his arms crossed over his broad chest.

"What? Don't you like my room?" I say.

He gestures across the hall. "Your room is over there."

"Azem, your mom went to a lot of trouble to put this together for me. I can't refuse her gift."

"You can use the room to blot your gloss, and to put on powders or whatever, but you live over there."

He's got his thumb jacked behind him. The corners of my lips curl. He's sexy when he's jealous.

"Will you please help me bring my bags down?"

"Absolutely, but I'm putting them over there." He says.

"Then I'll bring them down myself." I try to leave the room, but Azem doesn't budge.

I slip my brand new piano key black iPhone out my back pocket. "Should I text Zara, to see what she has to say about it?"

Azem's vein pops out at his temple. He doesn't look at me as he steps to the side.

Azem takes all my bags out of the truck and puts them in the hallway. He looks at me for a long time before he moves the bags into my room.

Unpacking all this stuff tonight is not happening. The best I can do is find pajamas, undergarments, shoes, and clothes for school tomorrow.

Azem disappears somewhere.

I'm tempted to look for him, but I'm desperate to wash this day off of me. I can't shower fast enough. Azem's still nowhere to be found when I'm finished.

Azem was not kidding when he said he could replace everything in my room. I doubt he had this particular set up in mind.

I almost get in the bed, when I notice a sliver of light coming from a cracked door further down the basement hall. I creep down the hall and nudge the door open a little but more.

Inside the room Azem's on the floor performing what I assume are Calisthenics. In the setting of this room, Azem's body looks even more ripped. It's easy to take his perfect body for granted when he's walking around in life. As he pulls his body weight up and over a high bar until the bar hits at his waist, I realize how much of a beast he is. He's performing moves that are so explosive, that I don't know how anyone can gain enough strength to do them. Every exercise he does is extreme. I can't take my eyes off of him. This is by far the sexiest thing I've ever seen.

"Come here," Azem calls out for me during a set of twisted plank pushups. My eyes are glued to him as his body twists from side to side above the ground. I want him to do that move on me. Right now. He looks up at me. "This is what I do when I miss you at night."

Sweat drips off his hair and body to the padded floor. He stands up and whips his hair back. Sweat flies everywhere. He laughs at me while I wipe the sweat off my arms and face.

I follow him to his room.

His brow furrows. "I thought you were sleeping in your room tonight." He says.

"Can't I visit?" I tease.

Azem cuts his eyes at me when he exits out of his bathroom. Azem prefers to air dry after a shower. Seeing him pace around his room naked is like watching living art.

"Can I move back in?" I say.

He sits one cheek on his dresser and faces me. "You never moved out." He informs.

"What do you call the room across the hall then?"

"Call it what you wish, but you live over here," Azem says.

"I love you," I say.

Azem closes the distance between us.

In bed, I hold on to Azem like I never have before. I'm so in love with him that I can't speak. A tear slides down my cheek when he slides my engagement ring back on my finger.

About The Author

This part of the novella is the most difficult to write. I am a wife and mother of two. We have a ten-year-old cat, which we can't fathom life without. Nothing you haven't heard before, right? Instead of going on about my home in the Midwest and my obsession with Zumba, I'll leave you with my favorite poem. It does a much better job of describing me. My hope is that you will fall in love with it too.

Thank you for reading my novella. Your time is a gift that I am ill-equipped to repay, but will forever be grateful.

The little cares that fretted me,
                    I lost them yesterday,
Among the fields, above the sea,
                    Among the winds at play,

Among the lowing herds,
                    The rustling of the trees,
Among the singing of the birds,
                    And humming of the bees,

The foolish fears of what might pass,
                    I cast them away,
Among the clover-scented grass,
                    Among the new mown hay,

Among the hushing of the corn,
                    Where the drowsy poppies nod,
Where ill thoughts die and good are born,
                    Out in the fields with God.

- Louise Imogen Guiney (1861-1920)

Check out *Part 1* of my previous novella, ***Bad On Paper***.

Made in the USA
Monee, IL
25 February 2024

54094581R00046